These exquisitely written, intelligently compressed stories are filled with characters on precipices, navigating borders of disillusionment and despair. I was transfixed by them all. This book is pure heart.
—Peter Kispert, author of *I Know You Know Who I Am: Stories*

In this collection of beautifully crafted stories, acclaimed poet Lee Ann Roripaugh captures the fractures and silences in ordinary relationships. Her characters quietly fight to hold onto their footing in relationships fraught with tension. A young girl struggles with her controlling parents; another story echoes this fight when an adult daughter tries to understand her controlling and mentally incompetent mother. After listening to her Beloved promise to leave his wife over the course of several stories, a woman finally charts her own course. Roripaugh's deadpan, incisive observations and her surprising turns of phrase make these stories shimmer. They will linger for a long time.
—Geeta Kothari, author of *I Brake for Moose and Other Stories*

In luminous prose, Lee Ann Roripaugh's *Reveal Codes* dissects relationships and contemplates what people owe one another. Roripaugh examines the loneliness of contemporary life, the desire to be seen and understood by lovers and family, and the ease with which expectations and hopes can be crushed. *Reveal Codes* allows readers a glimpse into the secret interior worlds of its protagonists and shows the complex calculus required not just to get along but to survive relationships. These stories are filled with exquisite imagery that reveals moments of surprising beauty against a backdrop of loss and sadness. This book is sharp and insightful and smart, a truly masterful collection of short fiction.

—Karin Lin-Greenberg, author of *You Are Here*

The stories in Lee Ann Roripaugh's *Reveal Codes* are filled with disappointed parents and disconnected lovers, revealed with a poet's precision for the language of heartbreak and longing. Yet through all the disappointments in these seventeen stories, our characters—through wicked humor and sharp observation—discover hope, redemption, and even acceptance in the simple, urgent gestures that make their lives complete. Each story closes with a scene that will expand the reader's heart, lingering long after the moment ends. This is a wondrous collection of stories from a writer who animates ordinary lives with extraordinary force and grace.

—Michael Nye, author of *Until We Have Faces*

# REVEAL CODES

Lee Ann Roripaugh

moon city press
Department of English
Missouri State University

*The 2022 Moon City Short Fiction Award*

MOON CITY PRESS
Department of English
Missouri State University
901 South National Avenue
Springfield, Missouri 65897
www.moon-city-press.com





First Edition

Published by Moon City Press, Springfield, Missouri, USA, in 2023.
Manufactured in the United States of America.

Library of Congress Cataloging-in-Publication Data

Library of Congress Control Number: 2023948963
Roripaugh, Lee Ann, 1965-
Reveal Codes

Further Library of Congress information is available upon request.

ISBN-10: 0-913785-84-9
ISBN-13: 978-0-913785-84-3

Cover designed by Shen Chen Hsieh
Interior designed by Cam Steilen
Text edited by Karen Craigo
Author photo by Lee Ann Roripaugh

moon city press
Department of English
Missouri State University

# CONTENTS

*For all the things revealed and all the things left unrevealed.*
*For emojis, semaphores, and signs.*

*For the shimmering revelations of biosemiotics:*
*chromatophores, pheromones, and phosphorescent signals.*

*For adopted sisters, chosen family, and best friends.*

*For all of my many wonderful colleagues and students*
*at the University of South Dakota, the University of Nebraska*
*MFA in Writing, and the Carlow University MFA in Writing,*
*with much gratitude for your inspiration and community.*

*For all of the mentors, editors, journals, presses, and reading*
*venues who have supported my work over the years with such*
*kindness and generosity.*

*For Nobu, Aiko, Nanami, Kuzuri, Yuki, Tampopo, Genji, Muku,*
*Kenji, Ten-chan, and Kumo.*

*And, with love always, for my Bee Bee Pie.*

*I would also like to thank the Wurlitzer Foundation, Hedgebrook,*
*Willapa Bay AiR, the Women's International Studies Center*
*at Acequia Madre House, the Brush Creek Foundation for the Arts,*
*the Bunnell Street Arts Center, the South Dakota Arts Council,*
*the Banff Centre for the Arts, the Kimmel Harding Nelson Center*
*for the Arts, and the University of South Dakota for the gifts*
*of funding, time, space, and support, without which this book*
*would not be possible.*

# REVEAL CODES

# Date

Fuji Bay in Sioux City, slow Monday night, and *The Bachelorette*'s on TV. She's stopped on her way back from the airport in an attempt to self-soothe with sushi. Earlier in the day, she said goodbye to The Beloved in a different airport, then dozed on and off through two uncomfortable legs. Saying goodbye to The Beloved is always dreadful. She feels it coming on as early as the day before—a red spread of despair, like acid on litmus, and by the time they arrive at the airport her chest is clenched into a tight fist of misery and she feels sick to her stomach.

On the flat screen mounted high in the corner behind the hostess stand and cash register, a woman in a shiny dress sits in candlelight at an outdoor table with a man whose head is meringued with too much hair product. Shiny Dress's blond hair riffles as if to imply the presence of an ocean breeze somewhere slightly off camera. Meringue Head says something awful to Shiny Dress. She can tell it's awful by the way Shiny Dress's smile slides off her face and falls into her salad like a sad little crescent of avocado. She can tell by the way Shiny Dress—bless her heart—attempts to save face by pretending to laugh, by continuing to flirt, even though her eyes are now somewhere else. Turned inside herself, maybe. They are the eyes of something crouching, something watchful and vigilant. She's glad the sound's turned down so that she isn't able to hear the awful thing Meringue Head has said to Shiny Dress.

The restaurant is empty except for a couple seated to her left. The man wears a blue Anderson Heating & Cooling shirt. The woman has a red tattoo on her forearm that says TRUST. When Trust gets up to use the restroom, she notices there's a man's face tattooed on Trust's shoulder blade: dark-haired, Latinx, mustached. She can't tell if the face belongs to Anderson Heating & Cooling or not. She wonders which thing is more awkward: having your face tattooed on your lover's back, or having another man's face tattooed on your lover's back. On the way back from the restroom, Trust meets her eyes and breaks into a wide grin.

Sometimes she comes unraveled at the airport, sobbing, causing a small scene in the terminal—a brief moment of diversion for bored travelers otherwise tractor-beamed into their cell phones. Sometimes The Beloved cries, too. In general, she disapproves of unrestrained crying at sites of mass transportation. In fact, there are airports she now feels compelled to avoid due to excessive displays of emotion. Sometimes The Beloved, who is not a good flyer, shuts down and takes a Klonopin. Sometimes, she tries to pick a fight with him when he has shut down and taken a Klonopin. But trying to fight with The Beloved at the airport when he has shut down and taken a Klonopin is like fighting with tofu. Lately, she simply accepts his offerings of coffee or scones or croissants and tries to remain calm. It's not that she no longer feels like a wild trapped bird is trying to beat its way out from inside her chest; it's that it's simply too exhausting to allow herself to become emotionally scooped out to that degree—like a honeydew melon-balled down to its very rind.

On *The Bachelorette*, Shiny Dress and Meringue Head ostentatiously toast each other, then drink in unison from their wineglasses. Meringue Head leans in for a kiss. She doesn't think that Shiny Dress should necessarily kiss Meringue Head, and, as kisses go, it looks staged. Junior-high kids playing spin the bottle and clumsily sucking face—wanting to be seen in the act of kissing, as opposed to necessarily wanting to kiss the person they're kissing. Shiny Dress and Meringue Head confer for a moment, then awkwardly kiss some more. After that, they get up from the table and walk off set while holding hands. Shiny Dress's heels are too high, so that she gives the impression of simultaneously clumping and limping.

Trust has ordered sunomono with jellyfish to start, and the waitress brings out a small bowl of hot rice to Anderson Heating & Cooling. He liberally pours a salty spiral of soy sauce over the steaming white grains, then eats it with a spoon and the kind of attentive relish that makes the rice look delicious. They sip their cold Sapporos, and soon the waitress arrives with a platter of norimaki—Philly rolls and dynamite rolls.

At the airport, The Beloved says that now, more than ever, he feels a particular urgency to address his situation. His "situation" is how he talks about his marriage. "The other person" is how he refers to his wife. He used to refer to his wife as his "then-wife," but since she felt compelled to point out how misleading this was, he now calls his wife "the other person." He says he's going to get a Realtor. She wonders how long it will take—after returning to his too-many hours of work, to the daughters he parents with such care, to "the other person" who leaves chicken breasts in the trunk of their car until the maggots arrive—for him to succumb to the deadly torpors of his day-to-day existence. She wonders how soon it will be until he represses this particular conversation altogether. He's possibly the sweetest person alive, so part of her feels ashamed for having these thoughts. His sweetness is what makes him dangerous, though. He's the emotional equivalent of the La Brea Tar Pits, and so another part of her has learned to put on glamorous dark glasses and coolly observe the drowning of the mastodons from a safe distance behind cynicism's fence.

Stray salmon roe bob in her soy sauce like translucent orange buoys, and she fishes them out with her chopsticks and pops them one by one into her mouth. Shiny Dress and Meringue Head are now exaggeratedly cavorting on a beach somewhere. Shiny Dress wears a tiny orange bikini. Dolphins are involved. It's like a *Star Trek* holodeck. She wants to sneer a little at Shiny Dress and Meringue Head, but really, she's probably just as much of a cliché. What would her reality show look like? She'd probably have to wander around all day wearing a scarlet letter while the villagers pelted her with rotten produce. Her friends have started to become embarrassed on her behalf. Her Japanese Mother likes to tell her that she should star on *The Bachelorette*, but only after being on *The Biggest Loser*. Her Japanese Mother thinks this is hilarious.

Anderson Heating & Cooling has a small transistor radio attached to his belt. It plays Mexican radio. Love songs. He nods his head and whistles along to the tunes. Occasionally he sings parts of the songs out loud to Trust. When he does this, Trust laughs and sways in time to the music, snapping her fingers.

She says goodbye to The Beloved outside a pretzel stand at the Washington Dulles Airport. As soon as she saw the pretzel sign in the terminal, she knew he would pick out a pretzel for himself while she went in search of a latte. She liked watching how happy he was while eating his pretzel. He decides to go back and get a second pretzel before his plane boards. To calm his nerves, he says. He's broken into a cold sweat. He doesn't want to go back, he says. He's rocking a little and he's taken a Klonopin. She loves him more than anyone. Her last image of The Beloved is of him standing underneath the neon pretzel sign: His worried face under a neon pretzel. The neon pretzel under a neon halo.

# Moist Towelette

She's confused by her husband. How he loads the dishwasher is completely bizarre. He persists in eating the good cookies—the fancy European ones she saves for company—even though she keeps finding new hiding places for them. She's pretty sure he's been masturbating in the shower. On Sundays, he doesn't even want to leave the house. When he runs out of laxative powder, instead of just going to the Costco and picking up some more, he breaks open her stash of Metamucil gelcaps, stirs their contents into his orange juice while she's still asleep.

She didn't think this is what marriage was going to be like.

When she finds the package of moist towelettes in the bathroom, she thinks they're disposable bathroom cleaning towelettes, and for several weeks she uses them to wipe down the bathroom faucets, sink, and counter. When she learns she's been cleaning the bathroom with her husband's butt wipes, she feels as if maybe she really has no clue who she's married.

"Who would need to use a thing like that?" she repeatedly asks each of her three sisters on the phone, adding that the butt wipes actually made the bathroom faucets nice and shiny.

☾

Not long after the discovery of the moist towelettes, she decides she's divorcing her husband.

*I want a divorce*, she texts everyone she knows on her way into morning rehearsals at the music school. She's promised her husband to stop texting and driving because she keeps getting into fender benders, but since she's divorcing him anyway, she figures she can do exactly as she pleases.

She's divorcing her husband because when she came downstairs earlier that morning in a chic, dove-gray linen sheath dress—simply decorated with two adorable stripes of blue-and-yellow piping along the princess seams—her husband tells her she looks like a Ziploc baggie.

At first, she doesn't know what he means. "What?" she says.

"You know," he says. "Ziploc." He gestures at the piping on her dress. "Yellow and blue make green."

"What the hell?" she says.

"Aw, come on," he says. "It's funny."

"How is that funny?" she says. "I've been saving this dress for months. I'm meeting with the conductor of the philharmonic today."

"Don't you remember the Ziploc commercial?" he asks. "Yellow and blue make green?"

"Are you a moron?" she asks.

He stares at her blankly.

"That was Glad, you asshole!" she yells. "*Glad*!"

☾

Around 1:00 in the morning later that night, she's sitting on the living room floor in her empty condo, now on the market, wearing her wedding veil and tiara—chain-smoking and drinking cabernet straight out of the bottle. She's left her husband. She's waiting for him to notice, but has a sinking feeling maybe he's just gone to bed instead.

Earlier in the evening, she returned from her meetings and rehearsals and prepared an elaborate meal. Her mother's always telling her the way to a man's heart is through his stomach and not his penis. Although she used to consider this advice retrograde and suspect, she thinks that if her husband thinks she looks like a Ziploc baggie, maybe she needs to assert a stronger grip on his heart.

Her husband, though, is golfing with his buddies. Then he goes out for drinks with them. He doesn't tell her he's not coming home for dinner. Her shrimp etouffee cools while she waits and fumes.

"How can I be a golf widow already when we've only been married for four months?" she demands when he walks in the door.

"Golf widow?" he says. "Have you been talking about me to your family again?"

"Don't you start with my family," she says.

"But they're nuts," he says. "Asian busybodies."

"You come from a broken home," she says. "You don't know what you're talking about."

"Here we go," he says.

"Why am I even cooking for you?" she asks.

"I thought you said I was an asshole," he says. "Why are you feeding me?"

"Bad answer," she says and starts to clear the table—throwing away the uneaten meal, dishes and all, into the trash.

"Have you lost your mind?" he asks.

When she's done clearing the table, she fills several large Hefty bags full of groceries from the refrigerator and the kitchen cupboards.

He watches her for a while, taken aback, then goes down to the basement to skulk.

She drags the heavy trash bags out to the curb, one by one. Then she stuffs her wedding veil and tiara, along with her best jewelry, into her music bag and drives over to the condo where she lived before she was married.

It's possible they're not really fighting about food. Or how to load the dishwasher. Or Metamucil. It's possible they're really fighting about money. About time and space. About whether or not to have a baby. They're both in their late thirties, and neither one of them has ever lived with anyone else before. They're giddy with the excitement of no longer having to stew in their own juices. Dizzy with the possibility of not having to be solely liable for all the shit that goes wrong. They're like heat-seeking missiles of blame.

When she runs out of cigarettes and wine, she calls her husband, tells him she's drunk, asks if he'll come pick her up.

"Sure," he says. He's good that way. "Where are you?" he asks. It's obvious he was asleep.

At home they have exhausted sex. When she falls asleep, she dreams she's living in a boardinghouse. Her husband's not there and she's trying to pick up his clothes, which are infinitely strewn all over the property: socks and underwear and tees. There are security cameras everywhere. She covers one up with a dish towel so she can masturbate, but she gets caught. A security guard arrives and promises not to tell anyone, but only in exchange for sex. There are elaborate negotiations over an expired condom.

The dream follows her throughout the rest of her day like a weird haze of smog. It still lingers when she goes into the music school to attend a recital—a gala concert celebrating the composer John Cage's one-hundredth birthday, curated by one of her friends from the musicology department.

*People are so random*, she thinks to herself throughout the hour-long performance of Cage's music: *4'33"*, *Sonatas and Interludes*, *Aria*, *Variations III*, and the Number Pieces. *Everything's so uncertain*, she thinks.

There's a reception in the lobby following the recital. There's coffee, punch, and photo cookies frosted with images of John Cage's face—bearded, open-mouthed, laughing. Watching John Cage's face disappearing into the faces of her colleagues and students, she suddenly feels a little bit lightheaded, a little bit queasy.

She wants to seek out all of the people in the lobby who are married or partnered. "Are you lonely in your marriage?" she wants to ask each and every one of them.

She's worried she's going to be sick.

All around her, everyone eating John Cage's face: Someone bites into his forehead, another nibbles on his beard, John Cage's mouth magically vanishing deep inside the strange cave of another person's mouth.

# Hello Kitty Head

When the hotel maid walks into their room, he is on top of her and she is about to come. He stops, spread-eagling himself to cover her.

"Um?" he says over his shoulder. "I think we're busy now?"

They have a weird history of exposing themselves to hotel staff.

The first night's always the best night—too early for her to begin asking difficult questions, too early for him to feel sad he doesn't have good answers. On this night, after they dress themselves, they go out for a late dinner: sushi and cucumber martinis. She knows he goes to make her happy, since fish makes him go into anaphylactic shock.

Later, she discovers he talks in his sleep if she asks him questions as he's dozing off. She finds it helps if she tugs on his beard.

"Do you know what pictures you want to use?" he mumbles.

"Pictures?" she asks.

"For your dim sum," he says.

She's delighted by this. He's like a conceptual poetry machine. A surrealist text generator.

"Let's just focus on one movie at a time," he mutters after a pause.

"Which movie?" she asks.

"The one where they fired all the cashiers at the Apple store," he says. "They were making the customers do all the work."

"Were we customers?" she asks.

"Yes," he says. "We were distributing tea tree oil."

Sometimes he wakes himself up midsentence, laughs sheepishly.

"Were you extracting text from me again?" he asks.

Sometimes she tries not to have any difficult questions. Sometimes she tries to let everything else go, to simply be happy in the moment. But sometimes, none of what they're doing makes sense to her, and her head becomes an elaborate hive of smoke-furied bees.

"Do you think the dream you had about us having sex on a bed in front of the open glass windows of an Apple store while people walked by and stared at us was in any way about *transparency*?" she asks.

"Maybe," he says.

"Maybe?" she asks.

"Probably," he says. "Or that Apple's evil," he adds.

"No one's making you consume an evil apple," she says. "I just want to be happy."

"I want you to be happy, too," he says.

"How about you?" she asks. "Don't you want to be happy?"

"It's hard to allow myself that," he says.

"Is that why we always end up naked in front of hotel staff?" she asks.

☾

At the Rite-Aid on their last night together, they pick up Coke Zeroes for her and Red Bulls for him. When he sees her pause in front of the display of Hello Kitty marshmallow lollipops, he asks if she wants one.

"Yes please," she says. Hello Kitty glitters beneath a shiny veil of cellophane in sugary pink overalls. Orange button nose disarmingly low on her face. Yellow bow on her exceedingly large head. She is both adorable and revolting.

The next morning, before they leave for the airport, he suggests they eat Hello Kitty. She feels dubious about this enterprise. But he untwists the bright gold twist tie, unfolds the crackly cellophane, proffers her the lollipop stick. Hello Kitty's sparklingly naked outside her wrapper, pale and doughy as a newborn.

She nibbles gingerly on Hello Kitty's ear, but immediately feels stricken and hands it back to him. He makes a show of ferociously gnawing on Hello Kitty's head. She knows he's trying to make her laugh, but it's not funny anymore.

What does it mean for her, she has to wonder, to be with someone who doesn't know if he can allow himself to be happy? The yellow bow on Hello Kitty's marshmallow head's bitten clean off, along with half her face. The leathery texture stale in her mouth.

"Make it go away," she says.

"I'm sorry," he says and hides it in a hotel dresser drawer.

"Don't ever make me do that again," she says.

"Do you remember the time we went to the parking lot carnival and rode Moby-Dick three times in a row?" he asks.

"Yes," she says. "And then we went to the comic book store."

"That was nice," he says. "Do you remember the time we flew the kites?"

It was true, there had been kites in the park, just the day before. The simple pleasures of wind and string, of give and take. Nonetheless, the irises were all blooming too early that spring. Nightsticking their way up through the ground—perennially intrusive and perennially alien.

# Amphibious Life

It's been this way all summer—the hopeless, slow-motion feeling that you're sinking to the bottom of a deep and murky pond. People seem to be peering at you oddly, as if from a great distance, and even though they talk and talk, their words never quite seem to match the busy shapes of their mouths. You spend entire afternoons spread out on the hardwood floor, sweating and listening to the arthritic wheeze and gurgle of the rusty window air conditioner, arms and legs signposting four corners, as if you've been caught frozen mid jumping jack. You concentrate on the dusty slivers of light squeezing through the slats of the closed blinds. After a while, the cats come by to nudge you with damp, mossy thrusts of their noses—whiskers tickling your cheeks. There are two of them, both Siamese. They are all eyes and big, funnel-shaped ears, with intelligent triangular faces that make them look like B-movie aliens. It is calming, the way they keep the apartment constantly in motion, like a free-form mobile, prowling about randomly with their rolling muscular haunches and tall wiry limbs. *Aleatoric*, you think, like the music of chance. You like to imagine they are thin hungry fish.

In the evenings, from the front of your apartment, you can hear the familiar sound of Simon's ten-speed bike clicking and whirring up the street like the fluttering wings of a giant mechanical insect. Then the clank of gears and soft thud of rubber against wood as he lifts it up over the railing and sets it down on the front porch. This is your cue to get up off the living room floor. By the time Simon enters the apartment with the key you've given him, you will be curled up on the couch, pretending to be immersed in a book. You sense that Simon disapproves of your torpor and is unsure of what role he's expected to assume. Ultimately, though, for Simon, a vegan of almost pathological proportions, any malaise can be cured with the proper combination of organic food and herbal supplements.

"Maybe you should supplement with an extra cup of soy milk," is the sort of thing he likes to suggest, scrutinizing your pasty and listless demeanor as if you're some kind of a science project. "I think we should try to boost your protein intake."

When you first became lovers, you discovered that he surreptitiously tucked away vitamins into the front pockets of his jeans. Chunky, smelly, horse-pill vitamins, which he would sneak off to take in the bathroom before falling asleep. You used to find this endearing.

Simon is a graduate student in linguistics. He has a ponytail and long, sensitive toes that look as if they are capable of doing independently clever things. Simon seems to be perpetually attached to an olive-green Army-Navy surplus backpack, which contains books, notepads and a large shoebox. He fills the shoebox with color-coded note cards, covered front and back, edge to edge, with his meticulously spiked handwriting. Simon is in the process of assembling his dissertation from these note cards. He does this all day long at his assigned carrel in the graduate library, and on the nights he spends alone at home in his own apartment. Sometimes, after dinner, he takes out the shoebox so that he can fuss with his note cards. He whistles tunelessly and happily as he shuffles, reshuffles, and checkmarks them, occasionally selecting a few to stuff into his back pockets. You feel he does this with a certain amount of self-satisfaction, and maybe even smugness, but realize this might be unfair.

Like Simon, you, too, have a dissertation you're supposed to be working on. The title of your dissertation is *Manic-Depression as Romantic Aesthetic Impulse in the Music of Robert Schumann*. It has been weeks, though, since you last met with your dissertation adviser, Professor Dragorimescu, after she handed back the first chapter with a blinking, quizzical expression on her face. Dragorimescu, the lone woman faculty member in the musicology department, writes cryptically brilliant articles devoted to the deconstruction of subversive ideological subtexts in French Romantic opera. She is the sort of woman who can employ phrases such as "formal alogicality" or "ideological interpellation" without irony. Dragorimescu has a mother who is always phoning the office, causing Dragorimescu to lift up an apologetic index finger prior to embarking on yet another mysteriously elaborate discussion which is held in Romanian, for privacy. More and more, the constant interruptions come as a source of relief, though, and you pass the time by staring at the improbable presence of a stuffed armadillo which Dragorimescu, for unfathomable reasons, displays on a small, elegant table in the corner of the office. Even when Dragorimescu is visibly annoyed, making tiny rapid checkmarks around the borders of her desk calendar with precise little stabs of the pen, the Romanian syllables pour from her mouth throaty, dense, and lush, like cream.

You are well aware that your dissertation has taken a strange and not entirely appropriate turn toward the bizarre, but you can't seem to stop yourself from obsessing over certain inescapable details. The fact that Schumann flung himself into the Rhein, for example, and had to be hauled back out like a large, weeping fish. Whether or not his wife Clara was having an affair with the significantly younger Johannes Brahms. The tiny "F" inscribed in the bottom corners of his household diaries indicating each time he and Clara had sex. Why did no one come to visit him at the insane asylum in Endenich for over seven years? What exactly was cupping? Why the leeches? The fact that after Schumann's death, the doctors at Endenich immediately cut out his brain and weighed it. And which one of them was the actual beloved? Was it Clara, after all? Or was it actually Brahms?

"This is an unusual, highly *imaginative* approach," Dragorimescu said to you, not unkindly. "But perhaps you are letting your imagination get the best of you."

☾

On the nights that Simon stays over, you lie awake and wait for his lightly sweating plane of inner thigh to grow heavy in sleep against your belly so that you can finally disentangle herself from him. You put on an old bathrobe, pour yourself a glass of Two Buck Chuck, and tiptoe barefoot onto the front porch, careful to keep the battered screen door from squeaking on its rusty hinges. There's an emergency pack of cigarettes hidden underneath the black lid of your petite hibachi grill—Simon disapproves, and isn't above throwing entire packs away when he finds them inside the apartment—and you sit on the weather-beaten porch swing, smoking. Even at night, the humidity presses against you like a tangible presence, and in the absence of daytime traffic, the songs of crickets and tree frogs bloom large and pulsate incessantly around you. You smoke and squint into the murky interior of your apartment, where the motley assortment of mismatched furniture casts bulky, elephantine shadows in the glow of the single corner desk lamp. The apartment seems unfamiliar this way, as if you're peering into the interior of someone else's life. There are nights when you sit and rock on the porch swing until the birds begin to pick up their quarrelsome rhetoric from the day before, and in the silky gray light, you can see the raccoons waddling off campus, sleepy and fat from pillaging the dumpsters behind the student union.

One night Simon wakes up and comes wandering down the hallway to look for you. He stops and turns around in the empty living room, confused, then stands on one leg, sleepily using a long skinny toe to scratch the back of his other calf. In the dim light of the desk lamp, his pale skin gives off a cool blue, fluorescent glow, and the hollows above his collarbones and hip bones take on a sculpted, saintly air. The cats rub their faces and wrap their tails about his legs, rippling in and out like cream-colored ribbons. Simon doesn't know that you're outside smoking on the front porch, watching him through the window, and his body assumes the unembarrassed authority of someone who thinks they're alone. He retrieves one of his moss-green, terry-cloth ponytail holders from the coffee table and twists his hair up into a dexterous topknot, then rummages for something in the front pocket of his backpack. When he bends down, you glimpse the gingery tuft of hair forming a corona around his anus. He stands up and turns around, and finally sees you on the porch swing. He realizes that you've been watching him, and his penis grows heavy, ornate and Baroque, rising from its coppery nest of red curls to point at you like an accusing finger.

As Simon tells it, he stopped eating meat at the age of ten. He always recounts the story with a combination of relish and outrage. In fact, when under the influence of a couple beers, he's been known to administer it like a *coup de grâce* to hapless colleagues innocently caught consuming hamburgers and hot dogs during departmental summer cookouts. As a boy, Simon spent a week every July at his grandparents' farm in Indiana, where his family would gather for a yearly reunion. During one of these reunions, shortly before his eleventh birthday, Simon was invited to go frog-gigging down at the pond with his grandfather and several of his older boy cousins. At first, Simon said, he was excited—happy to be included, and exhilarated by the adventure of going out in the middle of the night. Simon was assigned the job of carrying the flashlight. His grandfather and cousins soon filled up their buckets with frogs they'd speared on the ends of their gigs like so many cocktail weenies on toothpicks. Afterwards, his grandfather built a campfire, and while Simon and his cousins roasted marshmallows on sticks, his grandfather cut the legs off each frog, one by one, with a pair of meat shears, tossing what was left of the body into the fire. A number of the frogs were still alive, though, and Simon said they began to pull themselves out of the campfire, painstakingly dragging themselves out of the flames with their remaining front legs.

"They were making some kind of noise," is how Simon always concludes the story. "I don't know what it meant, but there were sounds coming out of their mouths, and I could hear them."

Shortly after you and Simon began seeing each other, you quarreled when Simon insisted on ambushing some of your undergraduate music theory students and regaling them with this gruesome incident over a platter of chicken wings. You'd brought him as your date to a post-lecture reception held at Dragorimescu's house. The next day, as a perverse gesture of reconciliation, he dropped by your apartment with a six-pack of Rolling Rock, take-out cartons of Szechuan string beans from the Happy Wok, and a tin of frog legs with a bow on it. After apologies were exchanged, you peeled back the curl of aluminum to peer at the source of dissent inside the tin. In the end, you fed it to the cats, who instantly swarmed upon the gift—nosing the tin halfway across the kitchen floor as they alternately growled over, pawed, and devoured the glistening ivory flesh.

You and Simon have now been together long enough that you've become inured to the way he brandishes this grisly frog tale, wielding it like some passive-aggressive social weapon, when you're out in public. Although Simon likes to present it as a moral parable on the correctness of not eating meat, you believe that what he's really recounting is the story of how he became a linguist. In your version, the way that you tell it to yourself in your head, you can hear the squish-suck sound of Simon's boots in the marsh surrounding the pond, feel the cool steely weight of the flashlight and the schizophrenic zigzag of its beam glancing across the water. You can see how Simon at ten is bookish and shy, easily shocked, and you're touched by his innocence. You can't get past the incongruity of the marshmallows. Why the marshmallows? And you're mesmerized by the terrible beauty of the image of sizzling frog bodies inching their way toward Simon's marshmallow stick—their open glowing mouths, and the fiery, indecipherable song they sing to him.

On one of the nights when Simon is working on his dissertation, you go out to a club. You've begun to do this frequently, with a certain duplicitous pleasure. The band that's playing is called Smear. They're women, two of them former BFA students, with tattoos and dog collars, singing vehement punk-rock anthems about date rape and fellatio. You find this kind of music, with its numbing frenetic drumbeat and predictable clanging chord changes, soothing—especially in comparison to the uneasy and elaborately shifting harmonies of Schumann. His serpentine chromaticism, incessant key changes, morbidly recurring motifs, and constant upsurges, down surges—all that fussy waxing and waning—has begun to make you feel queasy and anxious. In contrast, the bands you come to hear at these grungy and smoke-filled clubs on the nights Simon stays at home in his own apartment are thrillingly loud and visceral. If nothing else, the sheer volume of noise makes you feel as if you've been at least momentarily jarred out of your underwater stasis.

At the club you see Miriam, the baker. You met Miriam at a similar club several months before, when Miriam inadvertently stepped on your toe in a crowded and jostling line outside the women's restroom. When your big toe had instantly swollen up like a prune, Miriam was contrite and apologetic. Since then, whenever you stop by the bakery where Miriam works, Miriam sometimes slips you a loaf of free bread when the manager isn't looking. As the weeks pass, the loaves—loaves so fresh they mist their plastic wrappers—become increasingly elaborate and exotic. Oatmeal and wheat bread dotted with plump sunflower seeds, a chewy white bread frilled with the delicate greenery of dill, a round loaf of Portuguese sweet bread with a glistening hard crust that looks as if it's been lacquered with several layers of shellac.

After the show Miriam invites you back to her studio apartment, where she uncorks a jug of cheap red wine and unrolls a sandwich baggie of gigantic pot buds like pressed, green tumbleweeds frosted with a sugary coating of crystals. The room immediately fills with the heady scent of spice and mint.

"I scored some Christmas-tree pot," Miriam murmurs with a shy smile. "I've been saving it for a special occasion."

When Miriam isn't working at the bakery, she writes articles for the local alternative newspaper, and the floor of her apartment is littered with papers, books and—quixotically—with at least three manual typewriters. Miriam expertly uses a pair of eyebrow tweezers to pluck off the potent red hairs, loading them into the bowl of a ceramic pipe. The pipe is in the shape of an anteater.

In the dim flicker of candlelight, you find yourself staring, after a while, at the sprinkling of freckles on one of Miriam's knees, showing through a hole in her jeans—it seems as if they begin to bulge and swell, one by one, into fan-tailed goldfish. Then, with a swish and a twitch, they shimmy away. When you try to reach out and cup one in her hands, it disappears. This is when Miriam stands up and unbraids the thick red rope of her hair. The curls on the back of her neck are slightly damp with sweat, and she's smudged in flour, the warm smell of yeast. Miriam is freckled all over, like a quail's egg, ginger and cream—from the broad planes of her shoulders to the cool pink edge of her areolas, across the lush curve of her belly into the crease of her inner thigh. Her hands are strong from kneading dough. She tastes of cinnamon.

Several days later, there's a tornado warning. All morning long, sinus pain circles your left eye with predatory intent. As the day wears on, the sky turns a queer mustard yellow, and by the time the tornado sirens begin their mournful cry, your sinus headache has grown monstrous and turned into a migraine. You pack up the cats into their cat carriers and take them down into the cramped, tiny basement of your apartment. It's more of a crawl space, really, with a trapdoor that opens up with a squeaky rasp on the floor of your back porch. Cobwebs stick to your face like spun sugar, and although somewhat cooler than the apartment, the basement is clammy, dank with the pungent smell of must. The cats, unhappy in the confines of their carriers, begin to voice their discontent, and their howls mix in eerie counterpoint with the circular wailing of the tornado sirens. The migraine comes in relentless successions of glittering, wavelike swirls, and you clutch your head as if it were a cracked egg, fighting down the nausea to keep the seizing yellow yolk of your brain from falling out of your mouth.

You try to keep your mind a neutral blank, because it hurts even more when you allow your thoughts to tumble around in the circular swish and wash of pain like socks in a dryer, but you find yourself haunted by images of Simon's frogs. Their moist and listless corpses seem to crowd around you in the dank interior of the basement, and when the migraine opens yet another piercing sliver of light in your skull, it's as if someone has clicked a slide projector onto a new photo in a slide show. You squint into the brightness, and see yourself, age eight, standing in the blinding summer light of your parents' backyard with a garden hose. You're surrounded by a circle of frogs—brown frogs with creamy tan bellies and mossy green frogs with buttercup-yellow stomachs. Plump, phlegmatic frogs with rolls of fat flesh dimpling at the creases of their arms and legs, and lean gangly frogs with long splayed toes. The frogs are all dead. Caught during a summer picnic, you've been allowed to keep them as pets for a day in orange Sanka cans with plastic lids punctured for breathing holes. The next day they're to be released back at the pond. Your father insists that they spend the night on the back porch, though, and by the next morning, sunlight has steeped them like tea bags inside the metal coffee cans. Their slick, limp bodies burn your fingers as you lay them out on the lawn, checking for heartbeats and studying their slack mouths, cloudy eyes. You spend the next hour doggedly sprinkling them with cold water from the garden hose, hoping they might revive.

Why haven't you remembered this until now? Particularly with Simon and all of his strident frog activism. But then you remember how you became so angry at your father, a gentle and quietly puzzled math professor. How you refused to speak to him, but instead subjected him to the snitty and infuriating brand of silent treatment cultivated down to a snide, fine art by eight-year-old girls. A few weeks later he was gone. Death by major appliance. You remember the terrible crash, the delivery man's shout, and seeing your father's eyes slowly film over, the line of his gaping mouth relax, as he lay on the basement floor at the bottom of the stairs—crushed beneath the refrigerator he'd purchased for the downstairs rec room. Your mother was at the supermarket. It had taken more than ten full minutes for your father to lose consciousness under the weight of the refrigerator. When the EMTs arrived, they managed, with the help of the delivery man, to remove the refrigerator, then applied CPR and mouth-to-mouth to the body for over half an hour before your father was declared legally dead. With a startling precision of detail, you can see the gracefully slanted script rising up like a silver welt from the avocado green of the new refrigerator.

"*Frigidaire*," you whisper to herself. "*Frigidaire*."

You have no idea how much time passes before you finally become aware that the tornado sirens are silent, that the sounds of wailing in the basement are emanating solely from the cats. You hear the muffled thump of a door shutting above, then footsteps creaking across the hardwood floor over your head. You hear Simon call out your name. You hear him calling for the cats. You gingerly climb back up the rickety wooden stairs, awkwardly burdened by the flopping rectangular weight of the cat carriers, being careful not to jar your painfully throbbing head. Outside the basement, the light is much too bright, even though the sky is still overcast. You let herself into the back door just as Simon reaches the kitchen. You realize that you're a mess—smudged and clammy, smelling of mildew and covered in a thin veil of cobwebs. Simon immediately takes in your painstakingly deliberate movements, the characteristic dark circles under your eyes.

"Another migraine?" he asks.

You squint up at him and nod your head.

"Oh, honey," Simon says sympathetically, "that's just so sad."

He's damp from rain, the hair at his temples starting to frizz slightly, and you can tell that he's boyishly excited by the storm.

"The power went out at the library," he reports. "Did you see what a weird color the sky was?"

You bend down to release the latches on the cat carriers, imagining that your head is a large Ming vase. Infinitely delicate, infinitely expensive. You feel that you mustn't let the water inside begin to slosh around. You must be careful not to let it break open. As you straighten back up, though, there's a horrible swirl of pain followed by an overwhelming wave of nausea, and you stumble around the corner into the bathroom, where you vomit over and over again into the toilet until there's nothing left but dry heaves.

Simon follows you into the bathroom. He stands over you and waits, and in between the sickness he hands you a cold washcloth. His kindness slices through you with a piercing, silver clarity. You feel impaled by it—paralyzed and unable to breathe. You know that in order to break through the surface of your silence, though, you will finally have to let go of the stony weight of all the secrets you keep hidden, even from yourself. You will have to give the secrets away, one by one. And even if it hurts him to have to hear them, the first ones will have to go to Simon. You will tell him about the frogs. About your father. About Schumann trying to drown himself in the Rhein and the dolorous gaze of Dragorimescu's armadillo. You will have to tell him about Miriam, and the compellingly lovely loaves of bread.

You pull yourself up into a sitting position on the edge of the bathtub and rest your cheek against the cool ceramic tile. You clear your throat—your esophagus feels raw, your lungs on fire.

"Listen to me, Simon," you will say. "I have something to tell you. Some of it will sound strange, and some if it you may not want to hear, but I need to tell you."

But first, you tentatively take a deep breath. And then another. Then one after another. And that's the real surprise—how easily it happens, the breathing.

# Semiology

At the hospital, the doctors say it's unlikely his father will ever be able to truly communicate again. The stroke's left severe lesions, they say, in both the Broca and Wernicke areas of the brain. His father's now drifting in an incomprehensible bubble of receptive and selective aphasia, they say. "Incomprehensible bubble" isn't quite how the doctors put it, but it's how he explains what's happening to his father when he speaks to other family members on the phone later that afternoon. Even though he keeps calling with updates and news, he's the only one who actually comes to the hospital.

Before the stroke, his father was a brilliant, difficult, and domineeringly articulate man—an incessant stream of scientific erudition and postulations, a font of strong convictions. His father used language as a verbal crowbar, he often thought, to pry open other people's craniums and pour in an unstoppable torrent of his own ideas and opinions. It was never the Mensa-caliber quality of his father's intellect that he found objectionable, but rather the inescapable intrusiveness of being *craniotomied.*

Several days after the stroke, he brings his five-year-old son with him to visit at the hospital. The boy has an encyclopedic knowledge of dinosaurs, which he likes to recite with obsessive fervor. A double-jointed scarecrow of a kid, he frequently seems to be auditioning for Monty Python's Ministry of Silly Walks. Sometimes he blurts out weird non sequiturs, such as: "Welcome! To the Kingdom of Meats!" Lately the boy's taken to carrying around a flashlight around with him everywhere he goes. When he approaches the hospital bed, he trains the beam of the flashlight onto the slackened side of his grandfather's face: the drooping taped-down eyelid, the downturned mouth.

"Stop it," he says to the boy.

"I'm saying hello to him," says the boy.

He steps forward to intervene. But then his father's left eye suddenly snaps open and the flashlight's unexpectedly snatched away by his father's good left hand.

The boy startles, looks up at him uncertainly.

He gently attempts to take back the flashlight from his father, but the old man's grasp is surprisingly strong. When he pulls harder, his father starts making a terrible sound—a keening, moaning oceanic sound, like a large marine animal in pain.

"Dad?" the boy whispers. "Stop it. I think you're hurting him."

He stops tugging at the flashlight and the moaning stops. "It's OK," he says to the boy. He wants to come across as reassuring, but knows he sounds freaked out. "Why don't we let Grandpa keep the flashlight?" he suggests. "I'll buy you another one," he says. "We'll stop somewhere on the way home."

☾

A week later, his father still refuses to relinquish the flashlight. The sounds he makes when hospital staff members attempt to pry it away are heartbreaking. Shower time is a nightmare. His father's moans and cries swirl and echo throughout tile and steam, making the staff and other patients restless and uneasy.

He brings a steady supply of batteries with him when he visits, since his father becomes bereft and agitated when the flashlight's beam goes dim. In a situation in which he finds himself stupefyingly helpless, it seems to be one small thing he can actually do for his father.

Late one evening, sitting by the hospital bed, he falls asleep for a while in his chair, then wakes to the bright beam of the flashlight in his face.

"Dad?" he says.

The flashlight beam swings around, bobbles unsteadily along the wall before glaring a reflective disk of light on the glass of the windowpane, then lurches around to the foot of the hospital bed.

"Dad?" he says, again.

The flashlight beam returns to his face and he squints into the light. Once again, it quavers along the wall before lighting up a sunburst flare on the window, then swings around to the foot of the hospital bed where it quivers on the brand name: SUNRISE.

"Oh, Dad," he says. "Oh shit, Dad." He's trying not to cry.

His father is a renowned biologist, famous for his discoveries in biosemiotics. He specializes in the communicative use of chromatophores—the pigment-changing and light-reflecting cells generated in the neural crest of embryonic squid. His father's work shows how squid are capable of manipulating their chromatophores for purposes of camouflage, group signaling, and to attract and seduce mates.

Although he's very familiar with the body of his father's work, he's always remained more responsive to the visual beauty of the phenomenon: the squid's rippling patterns of colors, the hot glow of phosphorescent bits of luminescence. At his father's urging, he pursued a bachelor's degree in biology, but in the end dropped out of grad school and signed up for art school instead. He earns a good living as an illustrator for scientific textbooks, making his own art on the side. His specialty is trompe l'oeil—illusions so photorealistically accurate they startle the viewer. He creates meticulously detailed representations of the natural world, then whimsically installs them into unlikely urban settings: a blue-ringed octopus swimming in the office watercooler, an army of jewel beetles marching down a concrete stairwell, luna moths in the subway. His work has started to develop a following, but it's an art his father—whose fastidious genius is intolerant of patterns that don't precisely mirror his own—has never understood or respected.

His father used to bring him to his science lab at the university on the weekends when he was a small boy. In retrospect, he wonders if his father was lonely. Or if he merely wanted an audience, a witness to his brilliance. He wondered if it disappointed his father that he always wished to be somewhere else—escaping his father's lab as soon as he could to restlessly wander the hallways or read comics in the stairwells. Once, he slipped into one of the entomology labs, where he accidentally knocked over a small glass vial of moth pheromones. When he tried to pick up the pieces to hide his crime, he got some of the liquid pheromones on his hands—the moth pheromones so powerful that even now, moths seek him out to flutter, lovestruck, at his fingertips. He never confessed, yet maybe the moths that started following him around everywhere he went revealed his guilt. Shortly after that, his father stopped taking him to the lab.

When he tries to tell the nurses and doctors in the hospital that his father is attempting to communicate with his flashlight, they either gently explain his father's condition to him once again or dismiss him altogether. But he keeps insisting. He's figured it out. All his life, he's wanted to understand and be understood by his father, and for the first time, he feels as if he finally knows his father's semaphore.

He spends so much time at the hospital his wife suggests that maybe he should consider seeing someone.

At first he's confused and doesn't understand what she means. "See who?" he asks.

"Like maybe a therapist?" she says.

He sits with his father late into the night while his father wields his flashlight in the dark in a triangulation of glancing light: his son's face, false sun in the window, the blue letters spelling SUNRISE on the foot of his hospital bed. One night a Miller moth, wings purring, nudges its velvety thorax against his fingertips, then becomes confused by the bright circle of light his father's momentarily trained on the window and hurls itself into the glass with the soft pop of an exploding popcorn kernel.

Most recently, not that long before the stroke, his father discovered that compromised or vulnerable squid light up their chromatophores and bioluminesce. They did this, he hypothesized, in order to disguise themselves as sunlight to potential prey below.

The squid turned themselves into *sunlight*, he said, in order to camouflage themselves and disappear.

# Belljarred

At fourteen, you were completely obsessed with *The Bell Jar*. Of course, you loved the wry, fucked-up voice of Esther Greenwood, but mostly you were obsessed with the way the book so coolly articulated the possibilities of an exit strategy. You didn't know anything about *exit strategies* at fourteen, but when you first heard the term, you immediately recognized the image of your fourteen-year-old self-searching for a neon beacon reading EXIT in molten red letters at the end of a smoke-filled hallway.

Your fantasies for escape started out small: running away from home and hiding inside the fine arts building at the university where you took your weekly piano lessons, for example. You imagined yourself sleeping in the women's bathroom, eating out of the vending machines. Or you imagined being adopted by the funny, always-beaming clarinet professor who said you were a piano *genius* and called you *kiddo*. His daughter was in the class ahead of you at high school and she seemed happy, popular, well-adjusted.

It was the *smallness* of your fledgling exit strategies, though, that made them completely unrealistic, you realized. Like *The Boy in the Plastic Bubble* starring John Travolta, you needed to escape the airless gerbil ball of your toxic sphere.

How you thrilled when you read, for the very first time, the passage in which Esther Greenwood insisted to herself that despite what her fiancé Buddy Willard's mother said about women needing to be the place that arrows shot out *from*, she, Esther, wanted to be *the arrow* instead! It reminded you of the rockets launching on television from Cape Canaveral and exploding through the Earth's atmospheric layers—troposphere, stratosphere, mesosphere, thermosphere, ionosphere, and exosphere—and breaking all the way into the rarefied alien air of *outer space*!

Your own mother was similarly fond of pseudo-sexual militaristic metaphors. For example, her code word for your father's genitalia was *cannon*, which you thought was horrible and gross. And after you were molested by the boy who lived across the street, your mother told you that your *submarine was sunk* and said you must never, ever tell anyone about how your *submarine was sunk*.

Anyways. Maybe it was because your *submarine was sunk*, but one of the parts of *The Bell Jar* you were particularly obsessed with was Esther Greenwood's intricate machinations to rid herself of her virginity. You obsessively read and reread the account of her semi-sordid, borderline-abject interlude with Irwin, the math major, with riveted fascination. And because your virginity was still technically intact, despite the fact that your *submarine was sunk*, you decided you were going to pull an Esther Greenwood and go on a mission to liberate yourself from the false and unfair moralities of your virginity.

An opportunity eventually presented itself in the form of the first-chair cellist from your high school orchestra. As an added bonus, having witnessed the first-chair cellist spin a donut in the high school parking lot prior to an out-of-town orchestra trip, your parents found the first-chair cellist unspeakably *loathsome*—so much so, they forbade you from ever riding in his car.

It's true, the first-chair cellist was, in fact, a complete *jackass*: a misogynistic born-again Christian with a gun fetish. But your parents didn't know any of this. All they knew about was the *donut*. Which they found *disrespectful*.

Your father, in particular, liked to shame you for being a crappy feminist anytime you did something silly, frivolous, or vain, but years later, you'd marvel at your parents' blatant sexism: all the girlfriends they prohibited you from spending time with because they said they were too "boy crazy" and sure to demonstrate "bad judgment," or the ways in which they wouldn't allow you to go somewhere by yourself but would give you permission to go with a boyfriend. What did your parents imagine was the *price* of that freedom? Anyways.

You were still fourteen, though, and not allowed to go much of anywhere with anyone, during the height of your *Bell Jar* obsession. What you discovered, though, was that your parents weren't comfortable saying no when it came to spending time with the sons of their friends or colleagues. A loophole! Which you learned to exploit. And because it afforded you an escape from your parents' house, where you existed as an unhappy paradox of crappy feminist/sunk submarine, you ended up spending a lot of time drinking coffee with two born-again Christians named PeeJay and Peter. PeeJay was the son of one of your parents' widowed friends.

At the time, it seemed odd to you that even though PeeJay was in college, so many of PeeJay's friends were musicians from your high school, including the first-chair cellist. Odder still was the fact that PeeJay's friend Peter, who was also in college, also a born-again Christian, was engaged to your fifteen-year-old friend from music camp, Nancy. In retrospect, you have no idea why your parents, who weren't at all religious (and who, in fact, denounced anybody who so much as even went to *church* as being a *religious crackpot*), didn't find PeeJay and Peter unacceptably *creepy*.

(There was another, similar loophole when you were a senior, involving Ben, the son of your father's department chair. Also inexplicable, because never mind *donuts*, while he was still in high school, Ben had been in a *legendary* drunk-driving accident—flipping his car over the bridge next to the Gibson's Discount Center. Ben broke his back in the accident and almost died. Ben had his own apartment in his parents' basement, where you spent a lot of time with your blue jeans down around your ankles, Led Zeppelin on the stereo, while he ate you out. His kisses tasted like Marlboro Reds and weed. You had a not-so-vague suspicion that the reason he spent so much time at the high school, despite having already graduated, was because he was selling pot to high school students. Still, unlike the first-chair cellist, Ben was—while maybe not the brightest bulb on the Christmas tree—goofy, open-hearted, sweet.)

So, anyways. After a lot of group coffee dates with PeeJay and Peter, you began accepting rides home from the first-chair cellist following after-school orchestra rehearsals. You asked him to drop you off at the top of the hill from where you lived so your parents wouldn't know you'd been riding in his car. Sometimes you made out a little first. You usually let the first-chair cellist make the first move, although he always ended up blaming you for the make-out sessions. Afterwards, he'd say that making out should only lead to marriage, and that he didn't want to marry you.

"I don't want to marry you, either," you'd tell him. "I don't want to get married at all," you'd sometimes add, which he seemed to find shocking.

Soon, the first-chair cellist began inviting you over to his house, which was across the street from the high school, during lunch period. His parents both worked, and the house was always empty. He'd take you to his messy room, which was bewilderingly arrayed with posters of Farrah Fawcett, a doe-eyed velvet Jesus, ham radio equipment, and back issues of *Guns & Ammo.*

It wasn't so much that you *liked* the first-chair cellist; it's that you found him *curious*. You were curious about what boys were *like* in the small mountain town where you grew up, and he seemed to be what a *lot* of boys—although obviously not all—were *like*.

On the day you had sex with the first-chair cellist in his messy bedroom in his empty house across the street from the high school, it wasn't so much that you *planned* to have sex with him, as that the conditions seemed *optimal*, per *The Bell Jar*. Opportunity: check. Squalor: check. Speed: check. Bonus points for discomfort: check, check, check.

All throughout that afternoon and night after having squalid, fast, uncomfortable sex with the first-chair cellist, you carried around a smug sense of having somehow broken out of the airless bubble of your bell jar, your toxic hamster ball. You felt a tremendous sense of *accomplishment*. As if you'd finally found a loophole! Into some tiny hostage crawlspace to wriggle in and bore through—bringing you that much closer to a glowing red EXIT sign in the dark.

The next day you weren't even a little bit surprised when the first-chair cellist informed you that what *you'd* done was *wrong*, that it was a *sin*. He told you that if you got pregnant, he wasn't going to marry you. You reminded him you were only fourteen and couldn't get married even if you wanted to, which you didn't. This just seemed to make him *more* panicky. He said if you got pregnant, he was going to run away and join the Army. You reminded him that you'd used a condom, which you *had*. You'd provided the condom, in fact, having stolen it from your father's nightstand while your parents were out grocery shopping. You'd been carrying it around with you everywhere you went, in case an opportunity to rid yourself of your virginity arose—a fact which the first-chair cellist misconstrued as being indicative of both sinful premeditation and vast sexual experience on your part.

Because you wanted the first-chair cellist to stop talking to you, you pulled out some prescription painkillers from your handbag. You showed him the vial of pills. For some reason, you weren't even sure why, you'd taken them from the back of your parents' medicine closet that morning. They'd been prescribed to you when your impacted wisdom teeth had been taken out. "Yeah," you said casually, even though it wasn't true, "I've been kind of totally messed up on these."

You enjoyed watching him go silent.

"I didn't know you were on *drugs*," he said. "You're really screwed up," he added. "I don't think I can help you."

"I wasn't asking you to," you said.

Later that night, before you went to bed, you locked your bedroom door, then swallowed down all of the pills, one by one, with a can of Tab.

You woke up late the next morning—literally, as if from the *dead*—to your mother pounding on your bedroom door. She was angry because you were forbidden to lock your bedroom door, and because you'd slept through your 4 a.m. piano practice.

"What's *wrong* with you?" she asked.

"I feel sick," you mumbled, and it was true. Your ears were ringing and your head hurt. You felt as if the simple act of speaking entailed fighting your way through a swaddling of heavy, woolen mummy blankets.

As you began to come to, your first thought was that the feeling you were having was *disappointment*, but then you realized it wasn't disappointment. It was something much more oxygenated and complex. Something weirdly powerful and full of a strange, crackly kind of rage.

You felt like someone had cracked open an air vent, like you could breathe again. Like you'd been fired into life and had managed to break the sound barrier. Like you'd maybe even broken through the atmosphere and orbited the Earth once or twice. So what if you'd come crashing back down into the ocean—space capsule ablaze and in flames?

# Meditations in an Emergency

The first time they're in NYC, she's kidnapped by a taxi driver who doesn't speak English. He doesn't understand when she tells him another passenger's coming. The taxi peels out from the curb. It rocketships towards who-knows-where.

"Stop," she keeps saying. "We have to go back."

"Mami," the driver finally says over his shoulder. "No English."

*Sweetheart?* texts The Beloved, who's come out to the curb to find the taxi gone. *Where did you go?*

Their room in Park Slope's awkward. They notice the two cheesy paintings hung on the walls are exactly the same, which makes them laugh and laugh. They eat almond croissants in a Hello-Kitty-pink Asian bakery. The Beloved takes her to the Frick to see *The Polish Rider*, because she hasn't been before and they can go for the first time together. They go to St. Marks and The Strand, watch a Harry Potter movie, eat biryani on East 6th Street. The next day, over brunch at The Smith, The Beloved tells her his therapist believes he's about four weeks away from finally leaving his marriage.

Earlier that morning, in the hotel room, she overheard him singing in the other room while she brushed her teeth. When he sings this song, thinking she can't hear him, it always makes her cry a little.

*Just a perfect day,*
*problems all left alone,*
*weekenders on our own.*
*It's such fun.*

*Just a perfect day,*
*you made me forget myself.*
*I thought I was someone else.*
*Someone good.*

*Oh, it's such a perfect day,*
*I'm glad I spent it with you.*
*Oh such a perfect day.*
*You just keep me hanging on.*
*You just keep me hanging on.*

On the train ride back to Park Slope that night, The Beloved becomes anxious. It's raining. The Beloved doesn't like rain. He says it's because his brain can't figure out the mathematical formula for how the drops are going to fall. As the train levitates on the bridge over the glittering city, he holds her hand and whispers baseball statistics into her ear.

The second time they're in NYC, they haven't seen each other in seven months—not since she broke up with The Beloved on the anniversary of the day they first met.

She knows how to make a point, The Beloved tells her ruefully.

They stay at Hotel 17, and even though it's the day after Thanksgiving, The Beloved cranks the air conditioner up to Arctic blast.

"I'm so happy," he says. "Let's stay here forever."

They order pork belly buns at Momofuku. They agree Momofuku's pork belly buns may be the most delicious in the known universe. They go to the *Chaos and Classicism* exhibition at the Guggenheim, where Jean Cocteau's *Blood of a Poet* makes them snicker. At the point in the film where the sculptor shoots himself in the head, then smashes his own statue with a sledgehammer, they're almost beside themselves with laughter. Other museumgoers start to give them stink-eye, so they continue circling the nautilus spiral. On the taxi ride to LaGuardia, the driver asks if they're returning from their honeymoon.

"Not this time," says The Beloved.

At the airport, their planes are delayed because of weather. The Beloved becomes nervous. He says he hates airports. He frets about his flight.

"What's the worst that could happen?" she asks.

"There could be a psychopath on the plane who splits my head open with an axe," he says. "Then he'll massacre all the other passengers before the plane goes down in an apocalyptic ball of flame, destroying an entire town."

They get coffee, share a chocolate croissant, wave at a cute baby.

"I want to have another baby!" The Beloved exclaims.

She stares at him. He's caught her off guard.

"With whom?" she asks.

"With you, silly!" he says, though now he's starting to sound unsure of himself.

"But you're married to somebody *else*," she says.

"I always say the wrong thing," he says. He shuts down and takes a Klonopin. There's an emergency at work. He replies to emails on his phone. She hears him humming softly under his breath.

> *I'm a loser, baby*
> *so why don't you kill me.*

When he gets called for standby on an alternate flight, they hastily say goodbye. Around 9 p.m., her delayed flight's canceled and she's rebooked for the first flight out early the next morning.

It's already late, so she decides to spend the night at LaGuardia. She texts all her friends, East Coast to West Coast, until one by one, they go to bed. She asks one of her former lovers in the city to come meet her for coffee, but he's still pissed at her, and hangs up the phone. At 1 a.m., TSA employees lock down the gates, herding stranded passengers toward the Au Bon Pain in the main terminal. An airport employee smokes a joint in the shelter while she waits for the shuttle. Homeless people sleep under newspapers on benches just inside the main terminal doors.

After eating some soup, she unpacks her camera. She takes a picture of a young woman in the yellow glare of Au Bon Pain. The woman wears a plaid hat and sleeps with her head on the table, using her black duffel bag as a makeshift pillow. The woman's baby naps by her side in a stroller. A yellow balloon floats up like an unexpected song, tethered to the stroller on the end of a blue ribbon.

She calls this picture "Yellow Balloon."

The last time they're in NYC they spend the first night walking around the neon fanfare of Times Square. When she gets overstimmed, The Beloved puts her in a cab and takes her to eat tong shu at Just Sweet. The next day they go to St. Marks and The Strand. They buy comics at Forbidden Planet. At the Kid Robot store, they leave with ridiculous amounts of urban vinyl, then sit on a bench on the median of West Houston, traffic streaming by on either side, opening their blind boxes. She's partial to Tokidoki. He gives her his duplicates.

On their way to lunch at The Smith, they pass a brick building with a brontosaurus painted in a yellow halo on the side, its tail curled below a window. She tells him she wants to live in that apartment, encircled by that brontosaur.

It's summer, and they're seated at the front of the restaurant, which has been opened up to the street. People walk by with their dogs. It's a cute dog parade! She points out the dogs she likes best to him. He says her best laugh is reserved for animals.

He tells her this is the year he's finally leaving his marriage. He says they should talk about their plans. He says he wants her to come live with him and his daughters the following summer.

She doesn't have the heart to point out that they've had this conversation before. The first time she agreed to live with The Beloved it was a huge fucking deal. He lives in a city she's been known to refer to as Satan's Asshole. It was such a big deal she immediately texted her BFF to say she'd just agreed to spend the summer in Satan's Asshole. *I thought you hated Satan's Asshole*, the BFF texted back.

"So what do you think?" The Beloved asks. "Is this something you'd be willing to consider?"

"Of course!" she says, mostly because she loves The Beloved, but also because she feels pretty sure she's not going to have to move to Satan's Asshole anytime soon.

"Oh, you make me so happy!" he says, and they kiss in the front of the restaurant with the summertime NYC people and summertime NYC dogs streaming by. Their waiter comes by to top off their coffee, tells them they're his favorite customers of the day.

It's a year since their last visit to NYC. The Beloved calls her on the phone in the middle of the day. He's just returned from a consultation with a divorce attorney.

"I feel like I need to immediately repress the last hour of my life," he says.

"What's making you anxious?" she asks.

"I don't want to talk to the other person who lives in the house," he says.

"You mean your *wife*?" she says.

"Yes," he says. "What if she stabs me to death in front of our daughters?" he asks. "Or maybe she'll convince me I'm Satan."

"If you're Satan, we'll be the perfect couple," she says. "Since I'm the Antichrist."

"Please don't say that, Angel Egg," he says. "Stop saying you're the Antichrist."

"No one appreciates my Antichrist shtick," she says. "Even though it's my *thing*."

"Because Satan *sucks*," he says.

"Huh?" she says.

"Don't you know the Cub song?"

"The who song?" she asks.

"The Cub song," he says. He sings it for her. Slow and soft, over the phone.

*satan sucks, but you're the best*
*holy smokes, you passed the test*
*when i'm with you, i feel blessed*
*my chinchilla*

*satan sucks, but you're OK*
*since you came, things go my way*
*here tomorrow, here today*
*my chinchilla*

*one day i woke up and everything was beautiful*
*my troubles had all fallen out the window*
*satan sucks but you're divine*
*sitting pretty by my side*
*oh my, oh my, my chinchilla*

"Isn't that a good song?" he asks.
"Best song ever," she says.

# Breakup Blog

Before your girlfriend—the one everyone thinks is a boy—becomes The Plagiarist, before The Plagiarist, drunk on rum, starts complaining that neon tubes in restaurants are talking smack to her, before all the stuff with the blah and the blabbity blah, you used to drive to interesting or kitschy places on the weekends together: Spink Cafe, Carhenge, WinnaVegas, the SPAM Museum.

One Sunday you visit the tallest Queen Anne in the Dakota Territories. You wish you could say it was the exquisite woodwork, the original imported wallpaper, or the dual gas-and-electric chandeliers you remember, but it's actually the middle-aged caretaker, Tiffany, with her drifty eye and slurred speech, who steals the show.

Tiffany insists you view her caretaker's quarters as part of the guided tour. It's a bit of a low-grade hostage situation. The awkwardness of squeezing into the cramped studio apartment with its vintage hot-plate, duct-taped beanbag, and worn orange shag is only mitigated by the weird abundance of pictures of handsome young men now unfashionably handsome in a cheesy/porny sort of way. They smile dementedly from their picture frames, scarily baring their shiny teeth. Their hairstyle choices reveal a startling predilection for the white guy's Jheri curl. Most are wearing brightly Cubist sweaters of Heathcliff Huxtable-esque incandescence. You think the pictures could be headshots for cast members of *Up With People*, circa 1980s, or maybe evangelical pop stars. Are they trophies—a litany of Tiffany's former lovers? An obsessive shrine of Tiffany's D-List celebrity heartthrobs?

After becoming The Plagiarist, The Plagiarist blogs your breakup on the internet. This means each day The Plagiarist churns out purplish emo prose peppered with pathetic vignettes from your relationship. The blog's called *Breakup Blog: Tweezing the Shattered Pieces of My Heart Out of the Carpet One Broken Splinter at a Time*.

You have to hand it to The Plagiarist. Despite the icky title, it's a pretty snappy format. First The Plagiarist talks a lot about her feelings with both hair-shirt verve and martyred solipsism:

> *Now that I'm the object of your contempt, I sleep much better. I woke up today to God handing me a Death Baby instead of rocking me the way a father should. I have wanted to efface myself. My side is slit by the tight smiles on the lips of poets who have nailed me, silent, to a cross that is meant for a thief who has stolen more than words. When the thief comes in the night, I will cheerfully load him up with everything you ever gave to me: the Rothko dish, the coasters with the floating circles, the skeleton watch, the glass bird with a tiny red heart that will never beat.*

This usually ends up morphing into a very sad memory, chock full of ominous foreshadowing from when you were still together:

> *I remember, several weeks before we broke up, eating dinner at our favorite hole in the wall. How you first admired the begonia hanging in the picture window, but then you critically fingered it and pronounced it a fake before rejecting it.*

And then—either the best or the worst part, depending on how you want to look at it—the post concludes with a zippy little featurette called "Reasons to Get Over Her," in which The Plagiarist catalogues one new thing each day that's wrong with you:

> *Reasons to Get Over Her #27: You were always finding the fatal flaw in things, weren't you? Everything beautiful you scrutinized and pulled apart. I was just like that begonia, wasn't I?*

In less than a month, The Plagiarist's picked up a ragtag group of cheerleaders—dedicated readers who post supportive comments after each of her daily posts. For example:

> Anonymous: *Your ex is a fkn bitch! Your so much better without her! Your a great writer overflowing with 100% all natural talent God gave you. Its obvi to me your ex doesnt know her ass from her elbow. LOL!*

> Xena23: *The image of God giving you a dead baby is sooooo sad. It makes me want to cry. Nobody has the right to make you want to efface yourself. Know that your words are caressing the*

> *deepest and most intimate parts of other peoples souls. We need you to keep touching us deep inside with the gift of your words.*

You need to stop reading The Plagiarist's blog. Need. To. Stop. You know this. Your friends agree. So does your therapist. But it's like looking into the distorted mirror of the funhouse effect on your MacBook's Photo Booth: fascinating/horrifying/fascinating/horrifying.

You need to stop reading. Why throw gasoline on the virtual bonfire of The Plagiarist's emotionally manipulative self-immolation? The Plagiarist can track who visits her blog. In fact, you're the one who showed The Plagiarist how to install a sitemeter. Need. To. Stop.

The entries that upset you the most are the ones where The Plagiarist writes about seeing you around town:

> *The sound of you walking away so completely fucked me up for two days that I wanted to drink myself into oblivion. I stood behind you in line at the coffee shop and felt myself growing rawly transparent and disappearing when you walked off without a backward glance. And nothing will happen. Will you ever read this? Nothing happened so why not blot it all out? I am effacing myself, I have wanted to efface myself. Do you still hate me?*

It's worse when you see not only yourself, but some of your own images and words clumsily dismantled and reappropriated into the daily lamentations:

> *Your laughter in the restaurant today: high red bursts. What stars fall on you? Have you watched Orion discothequing westward in the ten o'clock hour? Do you twist your hair as you watch TV? Do your dreams have orchestra scores with violas and contrabassoons resonating like human voices? Are you haunted by the river, its hurry and eddy and snags, the sound of water flowing and fish plopping? Do you sit like the shadow of a bird on a wall as the lamplight keeps the terror at bay? Do your cats pretend they're in the circus, performing astounding feats of feline grace as they leap to catch Superballs in their mouths? Do you lose track of time when you explore the dictionary, page by giddy page? When grocery shopping, do you write poetry for the squash and apples? Will you tell me all your stories again? I was curled up in a rocking bed full of broken bottles, talking to what-never-did-exist. Sometimes all I do now is turn from side to side, not knowing my fate, or if I have one.*

Even worser:

> *I sit outside your apartment in my car, waiting all morning hoping to catch a glimpse of you. When you don't come out I go up the stairs and stand outside your door, listening for you inside. Your refusal to open a door that you slammed shut turns the interruption into a rupture. You are never so beautiful as when you think no one is looking.*

*Push me hard out of the cargo hold. I'm laughing, falling, and turning like a record on a spindle.*

This story isn't turning out the way you intended. This story's supposed to be funny, but instead it's making you very uncomfortable: that squicky mix, that vertiginous swirl of pity and umbrage, that accompanies any retrospective consideration of The Plagiarist.

What does it mean that you've lifted verbatim small chunks of The Plagiarist's blog? Are you trying to take back bits of yourself (fingernail clippings, strands of hair, the toothbrush's DNA) stolen under false pretenses and without your permission? Are you replagiarizing The Plagiarizer? Reblogging the blog? Retweeting the tweet? Rebreakupping the breakup?

Some people claim the birth of social media occurs in a Fabergé shampoo commercial. Remember the one with Heather Locklear? In the commercial, Heather Locklear holds out a golden honeycombed bottle and says: "When I first tried Fabergé Organics Shampoo with pure wheat germ oil and honey, it was so good I told two friends about it, and they told two friends, and so on, and so on, and so on." With each repetitive iteration, her face multiplies exponentially on the screen until she becomes a multifaceted prism of many tiny, polyvocal Heather Locklears.

Where are you even going with all of this? What meme are you replicating? What malware are you letting go viral?

☾

After the guided tour with Tiffany at the tallest Queen Anne in the Dakota Territories, you take The Plagiarist out for dinner. The Plagiarist drinks too many Bloody Marys and becomes increasingly grandiose.

You, on the other hand, want to go home and cut out the old carpeting in your bedroom, which smells funny and has been making you sick. The Plagiarist has been promising for weeks to help you. Unlike The Plagiarist, your work week's gruelingly full. Most of your free time goes toward trying to spend enough time with The Plagiarist to keep her happy.

Back at your apartment, The Plagiarist complains of cramps, then flops down on your bed and goes to sleep. When you try to wake The Plagiarist, The Plagiarist says she's getting up, then promptly falls asleep again.

Eventually, you give up. You move the furniture out of the bedroom by yourself. It isn't exactly quiet, but the Plagiarist sleeps through the entirety of the furniture moving and is still sleeping when you begin to X-Acto-knife the dirt-encrusted, mildewed carpet away in strips and chunks to reveal the hardwood floor below.

It gets late. You're exhausted and lonely. Lately, you've been starting to get the feeling that you might as well be dating yourself. The Plagiarist twitches, then rolls over and moans. Down for the count. All that's left of the carpet—you have by that time cut all the way around The Plagiarist—is a neat square under the bed. The Plagiarist drifts obliviously—a quiet hump in the arc of lamplight—crashed out on a sandy brown island of carpet bloodied with overblown cabbage roses.

That's when you realize you've just painstakingly X-Acto-knifed The Plagiarist out of your life. It will be months before The Plagiarist becomes The Plagiarist, before the full extent of the lies comes to light, the enormity of the emotional sustenance required to feed The Plagiarist's terrible piehole of inconsolable need. There will be drama and scenes and unlikely stories and outright lies, and at the end of it all, The Plagiarist will play her trump card and threaten to harm herself. At the end of it all, nothing you can possibly do for The Plagiarist will ever be enough.

Over the next few months, you'll repeatedly have to tell yourself it's not your fault you're on a plane spiraling out of control. Over the next few months, you'll repeatedly have to tell yourself to put on your own oxygen mask first. You'll seesaw back and forth between guilt and resentment like a glass-bulbed drinking bird toy dipping its insatiable red beak in and out/and in and out/of its diminishing cup of water.

But this. This is the black box that doesn't show up in the Breakup Blog. This is the point of engine failure. The tipping point, the straw, the ground zero, the—just for the record and in case you are reading this—the exact moment in which it all went down.

# But the Psychometric Assumptions of the Tool Were Grossly Violated

"Entomologist or exterminator?" he asks. The man from the coffee shop rolls her onto her back, takes her left foot into his hand, massaging the instep for a moment with a thumb, before hooking her leg over his shoulder and pressing himself deeper inside her.

His penis is vertically pierced with a large silver barbell that glints in the dark of her bedroom. It comes unscrewed like an industrial nut and bolt. He makes a production of revealing the quarter-sized aperture to her when he unscrews the jewelry.

(*Apadravya*, is what she comes up with when she googles the next day to see what's what. She's the kind of woman who likes to know what's what.)

"Entomologist," she tells him. "Duh."

It's a weird meet, not a cute meet. He sits much too close at the adjacent table, pulling his chair up so they're practically sitting across from one another.

He puts on a pair of glasses, begins scribbling margin notes in Deleuze. *Pretentious*, she thinks. She glances at his handwriting. *Serial killer script*, she thinks. He has multiple ear piercings: scaffold, pinna, orbital, and rook. He stares at her over the top of *Capitalism and Schizophrenia*. When she looks up, he laughs out loud.

"So what else?" he asks, as if they've already known each other for a long time.

When she mocks this exchange over the phone later on with the BFF, the BFF says that maybe she's being a little bit harsh.

It's true, the artichoke's her totem produce. It's true, she only likes men when they're a little bit damaged. She needs them to come with a dent, a ding, an open *wound* of some sort. Physical, or psychological, it doesn't really matter—although physical's easier to spot and saves time.

The man from the coffee shop keeps turning up. He's at the friend of a friend's art opening. He shows up at the cafe on the night when there's jazz. One Saturday night, as she's dancing with a crowd of women in a happy glitter of vodka and blues, she notices him standing outside. He's cleared off a view-hole in the misted windows with the elbow of his coat and he's peering into the long tunnel of the old bar's tin-roofed back room.

He keeps turning up. He lives in a faraway city, but he's in town house-sitting for his parents. He claims to be an epileptic, which she thinks might be a narrative garnish, but why lie about something like that? When his strangeness starts to become strangely appealing, she lets him into her bed. The last time she sees him he makes breakfast for her. He stirs pine needles from his parents' Christmas tree into the scrambled eggs.

☾

Every interaction, she thinks, is like one of those Russian nesting dolls. There's a moment she can always peel down to and pinpoint: the seed within the shell, the kernel within the seed, the tiny sliver of epiphany piercing the kernel like a splinter in the heart.

It's like dreading the eye puff test at the optometrist. She feels ridiculous later, knowing she's built it up too much in her head, but she can't help it. Because there's a tiny dagger of air. Being shot straight into her *eye*. When she places her face in the metal stirrup she tears up and flinches in self-defense. Then *POOF*! It's over.

"It's *OK* to like someone," says the BFF.

That seed within the shell? That kernel within the seed? That tiny sliver of epiphany piercing the kernel? This is that moment: thirteen below. They are standing outside downtown after last call and he offers her a ride. They drive to the cemetery, headlights combing through tangled curls of fog.

"I'm here for two weeks," he says. "Let's make plans."

"I don't like plans," she says. What she really means: *Last year I was in love, and it's not possible for the way that love ended to have been more awful.*

Inside his car, they tumble like socks in a dryer. The windows glaze over with a shiny rime of ice. She red-pens her number onto his hand.

The next day she notices the yield sign next to her apartment's been graffitied in black Sharpie.

She recognizes the handwriting. *YIELD TO ME!* it reads.

She walks past the sign every day—after he's long gone, after the cold snap breaks, after the fog has cleared. Even by the following summer, the letters still haven't begun to yield to the elements. *TO ME!* doesn't wash off. *TO ME!* doesn't fade.

# Reveal Codes

Every night, you come home around midnight to find Neurotic Cat Boy tractor-beamed to the SyFy Channel. His modus operandi is to procrastinate the entire day away, until he's worked himself up into a toxic froth of self-loathing. By the time you get off work, he's fallen into the paralytic stupor of pure despair.

"I suck," he says, as soon as you walk in the door.

"Poor sucker," you reply.

Neurotic Cat Boy's slender and awkward as a giraffe. He nibbles gently on organic produce and spends much of his day, when he's not in classes, reading the body language of your various cats in order to better anticipate their feline needs. It's become increasingly apparent that he's not cut out for the aggressive academic posturing of grad school. Neurotic Cat Boy's earnestly transparent in both his shortcomings and his insecurities. It's not difficult for you to envision the highly competitive students in the art history department sensing blood in the water when he blinks his long-lashed doe eyes and begins to stammer. You suspect his peers, and even some of his professors, too, are guilty of assuaging their even-deeper insecurities at Neurotic Cat Boy's expense.

"How was work?" he asks.

"Sucky," you say.

You work as a night word processor at one of the downtown law firms where your supervisor, Barb the Word Processing Manager, wields her petty tyrannies over the droning room of clicking cubicles with the zealous gusto of a passive-aggressive demagogue.

"By the way, the internet called. They've run out of stuff for you to buy," he says, gesturing at a small pile of packages from eBay on the kitchen table. "Ha ha," he adds, to make sure you know he's being mournfully droll.

Sometimes he tells you something cute or funny the cats did. Sometimes he tells you he's left a hot potato for you in the stove.

"Why do I suck so much?" he inquires plaintively.

"Go to bed," you tell him. "Suck less tomorrow."

It's not that you're unsympathetic, but you have your own problems. You've already completed your graduate degree and now, drowning in student loan debt, it's become apparent that typing's your sole "marketable" skill. Neurotic Cat Boy's seven years younger than you are, so you've already been there/done that. Sometimes you want to tell him that completing his seminar paper on psychoanalytic trauma and the use of meat in the paintings of Chaïm Soutine is the least of his worries. But you suspect that Neurotic Cat Boy, key witness to your awkward thirty-something flailing, already knows this.

You work in a skyscraper located across from the capitol building. You go in at 3:00 in the afternoon, then spend eight hours transcribing depositions from tape, putting changes into legal briefs, and decoding revised sections of real estate contracts scribbled onto yellow legal pads by harried, Type-A attorneys. At 8 p.m., there's a stressful flurry of activity to ready documents for the last FedEx pickup for overnight delivery, and then again at 10 p.m., for the last DHL pickup for overnight delivery.

Most nights you come home with an aching neck and a fisted knot clenched between your shoulder blades. Every once in a while, though, there's a slow night, and after Barb the Word Processing Manager leaves, you and the other night word processor, Lydia, forward the phones to the smoking lounge, where you smoke Marlboro Lights and gossip—the Midwestern city spread below you like a sleepy Lite-Brite board, cursor blink of cars crossing the Olentangy River bridge.

Lydia, who does most of the talking while you smoke your cigarettes, likes to complain about her husband, Miles, who can't seem to hold down a steady job. She says Miles is OCD. "I swear, he goes through several rolls of paper towels every day. I find them wadded up in the trash. We have to buy them in bulk at Sam's Club. When I get home from work, the entire house *reeks* of Windex. Breathing that much Windex can't be good for you, can it?" Lydia asks.

You agree that it probably isn't good. You tell her about Neurotic Cat Boy, who's paranoid about chemicals, and cleans with a T-shirt wrapped around his face. Like a *bandit*.

"Have I told you the latest about Roxanne?" Lydia asks. Roxanne is Lydia's daughter.

"No," you say.

"Her boyfriend quit his job and moved to Pennsylvania to be with her, and he's living with her in her dorm room."

"Isn't that illegal?" you ask.

"Probably," says Lydia. "Not to mention her grades are for shit. She's pissed at me because I keep sending her condoms." Lydia pronounces the "doms" in "condoms" like plural dominatrixes.

"Condoms?" you ask.

"Because if she gets pregnant and quits school I'm going to *kill* her." Lydia exhales a mournful plume of smoke and sighs. "Like mother, like daughter."

Each week is a muddled blur of bus rides, Cup-a-Soup, and the endless bony clicking of computer keys. The weekends are a different kind of blur: grocery shopping, errands, laundry at the coin-operated Soap-n-Suds, where you and Neurotic Cat Boy can have a cheap beer while you wait for your clothes to dry. Sometimes, if you can afford it, you go to a movie.

More and more often, though, you wake up in the middle of the night, pinned down by the hot weight of limp cats, riddled with anxiety, wondering if this is what your life is going to be like. Sometimes you study the familiar ridge that Neurotic Cat Boy's body makes in the bed next to you—he likes to sleep in the fetal position, with his head completely under the covers—and wonder what you're doing together. You feel an immense tenderness for him, as if he's a large jittery cat, but sometimes it just all seems so *arbitrary*. You suspect that like many other young artistic couples you're at loose ends in your lives. You imagine that you're huddling together in a creepy forest, like Hansel and Gretel, for safety. When pressed, you describe your relationship to others as being on a year-by-year lease, with an option to renew.

But even the sleepless nights are better than the ones where you dream all night that you're still at work. On these nights, you sometimes wake up Neurotic Cat Boy by typing on his face.

At work, there's a kerfuffle when Barb the Word Processing Manager discovers a sticky note in the morning clinging to the lip of her wastepaper basket with the word *earwax* written on it. Barb goes into a tizzy and insists on showing the sticky note to all of the word processors, demanding to know whose sticky note it is. Barb can't actually blame any of the employees for leaving the sticky note (as if she could blame someone for something like that) because obviously, any of the hundred-plus lawyers who work for the firm could have dropped it into Barb's wastepaper basket as well. But still, she won't let it go. Why would *anybody* write down a thing like that? Barb keeps asking. What could it possibly *mean*?

Later, on that first night of Earwax-gate, when you get home and tell Neurotic Cat Boy all about Barb and the sticky note, he seems harried and distracted. Plus, he's doing the purse-y thing with his mouth that means he's keeping a secret he wants to tell you but won't.

When you take a peek inside the oven, hoping there might be a warm potato inside, you find a Polaroid of Neurotic Cat Boy's penis instead. You slip it into your pocket without saying anything and go upstairs. In the bathroom, when you open up the medicine cabinet to take out your contact lens case, you find another Polaroid of Neurotic Cat boy's penis taped to your face cream. And in the bedroom, when you pull your pajamas out from underneath your pillow, you find a third one taped to your snoring fat black cat. You keep waiting to see if Neurotic Cat Boy is going to mention the Polaroids, but he doesn't bring it up.

Following the opening salvo of Earwax-gate, you and Lydia initiate a full-blown battle with Barb by leaving a cryptically inscribed sticky note in her wastepaper basket every night at the end of your shift, after the janitor's made his final rounds on the floor. Barb doesn't say anything about the sticky notes after the first one, though. But she keeps every single one of them in her upper right-hand desk drawer. You and Lydia know this because you check. Here is the list of words you've left:

*toejam*
*smegma*
*spooge*

*goober*
*felch*

When Barb informs the word processing staff that she's taking a week off at the end of the month to attend a Christian workshop on learning how to be more judgmental, you're unsure of whether to view this as a victory of sorts, or a setback.

At home, you similarly don't say anything about Neurotic Cat Boy's Polaroids, although you keep every single one of them in a Ziploc baggie that you hide at the bottom of a steamer trunk where you've been storing the secret stash of vintage marbles that you compulsively buy on eBay.

Weeks pass, and the law firm does a rollout of Microsoft Word as the new word processing software. You miss Word Perfect, in particular the reveal codes: being able to see where the brackets of boldness begin and end, the clarity of being able to distinguish a hard return (HRt) from a soft return (SRt). Weeks pass, and the Polaroids transform from dick pics into more elaborately costumed photographs: a torso, crotch, thighs, but never a face. First, Neurotic Cat Boy puts on your stockings, sometimes your bras and underwear, then eventually your lingerie.

"Are those my earrings?" you ask him one night when you spy a glint of sterling and amethyst as he pulls back his wavy hair into a man bun. You're at the late-night all-you-can-eat buffet at the Chinese karaoke bar, where you sometimes like to go as a treat after paydays.

"I didn't think you'd mind," he says. "Do you?"

You aren't sure what, exactly, Neurotic Cat Boy is asking, so you shrug and help yourself to a crab rangoon from his plate.

Any relationship, you think, is like watching the images surface on a developing Polaroid. It used to bother you that Neurotic Cat Boy never told you that he loved you, but lately, Neurotic Cat Boy's begun to feel more like a younger brother than a lover. Lately, it seems as if most of your conversations are held either through or about the cats.

"Tea-Head the Cat wants to know why I suck so much," he says when you come home from work.

"Tell Tea-Head the Cat to tell you to suck less tomorrow," you reply.

Later that night, after you've returned from the all-you-can-eat Chinese buffet and karaoke bar, after you've watched the episode of *Buffy the Vampire Slayer* that Neurotic Cat Boy has taped for you, after he's fallen asleep—wrapped up tightly as an enchilada in his protective wrap of blankets—you wonder, again, if you really *do* mind. You yank back the covers and wake him up.

"Oh, God, what's wrong?" he says. "Are the cats OK?"

"Why don't we ever say, 'I love you'?" you ask him.

"Well … um … what *is* love, really?" he stammers, even though he knows you hate it when he answers a question with another question. "What does it even *mean*?"

"That's what I want to know," you say.

He picks up the nearest curled-up croissant of a cat and holds it up in front of his face, like a cat mask, or a ventriloquist's dummy, before switching into the special cat voice you sometimes use together. "Tea-Head the Cat says that for better or for worse, for richer or for poorer, in sickness and in health, we promise you that you'll never run out of toilet paper again for as long as we all shall remain together," says Neurotic Cat Boy, in cat voice.

"*Seriously*?" you ask, nonplussed.

"Yeah," he says. "Is it OK if we go back to sleep now?"

You feel a strange queasy wash of something like vertigo. You wonder, who is Neurotic Cat Boy, *really*? Who does this stranger's face belong to, this face onto which you've been typing the unconscious language of your disappointing dreams?

# Semaphores

When your father becomes obsessed with the idea of turning you into a competitive swimmer, he doesn't ask you if you *want* to be a competitive swimmer; he just forges ahead with the plan. You are merely the body by which he executes his vision. One day, you're practicing four hours of piano a day, with dreams of becoming a concert pianist, and taking ballet lessons twice a week. The next, you're suddenly going to swim practice for three hours every night and coming home with hair crunchy from chlorine, too exhausted to eat dinner, your eyes swollen shut and bloodshot.

There are swim coaches, of course, but this isn't enough. Your father—despite the fact that he, himself, isn't a strong swimmer—insists on providing you with constant, one-on-one coaching. He makes you lift weights in the living room, sets up the Stylaire chair with foldout step stool in the master bedroom, and makes you repeatedly practice diving-block dives onto your parents' bed. He has you practice backstroke flip turns against the refrigerator on the kitchen floor until you accidentally slam your head against the kitchen cupboards. After the three-hour swim practice and cool-down, he makes you stay and swim 100-yard butterflies, full speed in order to try and beat your best time on the stopwatch. If you don't want to, he yells at you until you finally have to comply.

He sits in the bleachers by the pool during the entirety of every swim practice and devises a series of coaching semaphores: instructional arm and hand signals that you're supposed to "read" and follow in between each timed set of swim practice. Because you can barely see without your glasses, you have to cup her fingers around your eyes and squint in order to see what he's signaling. A crooked elbow raised high means you're letting your elbow droop and throwing your left arm around in the freestyle; a turned head with a hand cupped below means that you're turning your body around too much to breathe; a hand pressing down in front of the body means that you're not pulling hard enough with your arms. Sometimes he beckons you out of the pool to come to the bleachers for a lecture. You're required to go over to the stands and ask his permission every time you want to go to the bathroom or get a drink of water from the drinking fountain.

It's not that you dislike swimming, per se, it's just that none of it is ever your idea, or your choice. That, and you're never allowed to just be an OK, or an average, swimmer. Instead, you're always a *disappointing* swimmer, a *never-good-enough-for-your-parents* swimmer. You hate the humiliation of being yelled at and shamed for not swimming hard enough or fast enough. You're pushing herself to the absolute limits of your physical endurance not because you *want* to, but simply to please your parents. You resent the fact that—in addition to being academically and musically gifted—you're now expected to magically transform yourself into some sort of *jock*. Suddenly, you're team members with many of the people who relentlessly bully you at school. Suddenly, you're being bullied at swim meets by swimmers from entirely different towns across the state.

You've never been particularly athletic in the traditional sense, and your father says that it's important that you acquire *athletic skills*, that you need to be in *good physical shape*, as if dancing *en pointe* in ballet doesn't require any athletic skills, or strength, or conditioning. Your father has taken to frequently reminiscing about how he played football in high school. You read your father's signal loud and clear: what he really wants, in these moments, is a *boy*.

Perhaps what's strangest is that your parents, who aren't joiners, who normally verge on the antisocial, seem to enjoy belonging to the AAU swim club. They volunteer to help out at the swim meets: Your father signs up to be a lane timer (providing a backup time by stopwatch in case there's a glitch with the electronic touch-pad timer), and your mother types up and mimeographs heat and race results in the clerical pool. They host swim club meetings at their home, where your father offers to make everyone tequila sunrises in the liquor shaker, and your mother goes overboard with platter after platter of fancy hors d'ouevres. They enjoy gossiping about the John Updike-esque infidelities transpiring among the swim club parents, reserving special gossipy venom for Mrs. Sloane, first name Lila, with her *The Graduate*-inspired, Anne Bancroft-y, frosted, up-flipped hair.

Your father decides that you have a shot at winning the high point trophy in a "B" meet, and he enters you into the ten-and-under category in the meet. For weeks, he can talk of nothing else. The trick of the "B" meet is that you can't swim faster than the cutoff times for each event, and your best times are wavering right on the cusp—sometimes you're a little bit faster than the cutoff time, and other times, you're a little bit under.

When the weekend of the "B" meet finally arrives, your parents drive you three hours away to the small town where the meet is being held. Your father coaches and lectures and throws up an endless barrage of arm signals before each event as you wait for your heat to arrive. Your instructions are to win your heat, but without going over the cutoff time. But you choke—compensating in the wrong direction and coming in well under the cutoff times for most of the events. Your parents yell at you in the stands after each botched heat. The combination of pressure and public humiliation makes you so anxious that you end up stress vomiting in the locker room before each of your heats—a phenomenon that sticks with you during the remainder of your competitive swimming days. By the last event, which is supposed to be your best event—the 50-meter backstroke—you miscalculate the distance to the end of the lane and execute an illegal flip-turn before your hand has actually touched the wall, and you get a DQ: disqualification. Your parents leave the meet in complete disgust and berate you throughout the entirety of the drive home—complaining about the cost of the motel and your poor performance. They'd bought you a jade ring at a local gift shop the first night before the meet, and on the drive home your mother makes you give back the ring.

After the "B" meet, you think you'll get to be done with swimming—that your disgusted parents will let you quit, and leave you in peace to watch *James at 15* on the television instead of going to swim practice. Instead, you find the goalposts have shifted. Your parents tell you that if you beat Monique, Mrs. Lila Sloane's daughter, at the upcoming home swim meet, they'll buy you an extra-large stuffed animal of your choice. They know that you have a weakness for plushies.

"Can I have the giant lion from the downtown toy store?" you ask suspiciously, trying to hide the eagerness in your voice.

"If that's the one you want," they say. "But you have to beat Mudball."

Mudball is the name they've given to Monique, Mrs. Lila Sloane's daughter, because she and her mother tan themselves to a rich brown color on lawn chairs in their backyard every summer. Your parents don't approve of tanning. They don't approve of Mrs. Lila Sloane, who's having an affair with one of the swim team parents, a petroleum engineer named Tom Johns. They also don't approve of Mudball, who lackadaisically "loafs" through every swim practice but is fast in swim meets.

Still, you're baffled about why they focus so much energy on Mudball, who—like you—is only a nine-year-old girl. You and Mudball are in the same class at school, and are sort-of friends, in that your parents sometimes allow you to accept invitations to play at her house. You are forbidden from ever laying out and tanning in her backyard, but she lets you read copies of her mother's *Cosmopolitan* magazine that she's rescued from the trash and hidden in her bedroom, and she lets you use her Stridex pads, smell her Tickle antiperspirant, try her peppermint-flavored Kissing Potion lip gloss.

The next home swim meet begins with the swim team coming out of the locker rooms in their team suits and marching around the pool while the theme song to *Jaws* is played on a boom box carried by the assistant coach. When the heats for each event are first called, all of the swimmers line up in the wrestling room and are seated in rows of six chairs, ordered by swim lanes, which move up row by row as each heat is called. After the heat is called, the first row is led downstairs and through the locker room, and seated alongside the pool in metal folding chairs, until just before the race starts, when the swimmers are allowed to line up in their respective lanes: lane three for the swimmer with the best qualifying time in the heat and lane six for the swimmer with the slowest time in the heat. Before climbing up on the diving blocks, the swimmers give their heat cards to timers with stopwatches and clipboards. The timers' job is to record the electronic and stopwatch times for the swimmer in their lane, as well as indicate where the swimmer places in the heat. The winner of each heat gets a little blue ribbon, and the top six times in the event get to race for event trophies in finals, which are held at the end of the day.

It's the 100 IM (Individual Medley) and your last chance to beat Mudball. You are in the same heat: Mudball is in lane four, and you're in lane two. You're neck in neck at the turn after the 25-meter butterfly, but Mudball pulls slightly ahead in the backstroke length, and holds her lead all the way up to the turn in the breaststroke. Mudball's usually stronger at freestyle, but you're both tired after swimming three legs of the IM.

You think of the giant stuffed lion that you want so desperately, and you put your head down and—despite the burning in your lungs, and the fact that your arms and legs feel like noodles—you hold your breath as long as you can and finish off the remaining twenty-five yards' freestyle in a dead sprint, breathing only once after the halfway line in the pool. Maybe Mudball doesn't see you pulling even with her, or maybe she's run out of steam, but you somehow manage to squeak past her during the last couple of yards and hit the electronic timer almost two full seconds before Mudball finishes.

Your father is so excited that he grips you by the shoulders and shakes you before handing you a towel to dry off. Your legs are trembling when you sit down with him in the stands, and when you begin to hyperventilate, he finds you a plastic bag to breathe in and out of. He gives you a quarter so you can buy a much-longed-for candy necklace, and you happily gnaw the SweeTart beads from the elastic and dream about the giant, plush lion. You imagine sleeping under its safe weight, growing smaller, and smaller, and smaller, until you're just a bean-sized girl secreted away within its soft golden haunches.

When they go downtown to look at the plush lion, though, your mother hesitates. It's a little bit *expensive*. She feels that maybe they should *shop around* and make sure it's the one that you really *want*. It *is* the one that you really want, but you're told there's no hurry for you to pick and that you have to *wait*. The next time you're downtown and you beg your parents to go into the store to look at the lion again, it's gone. It's been sold. Eventually, your parents buy you a discount bear, but it isn't the lion that you were promised.

A couple months later it's parent visitation day at the grade school. The parents are coming to the classrooms, where they'll review their children's assignment books. You have a bad cold, and your parents write you a note so you can stay inside the classroom during recess.

You don't know why you do it. You really have no idea. But when the teacher and the other students are outside for recess, you go to Mudball's desk, quietly ease up the lid, and take out her assignment book. Then, with dark crayons, you scribble all over Mudball's homework. Mudball isn't a particularly strong student. Her homework's riddled with errors and misspellings, and sometimes it isn't even finished. But still, you scribble on all the pages anyway: serial-killer black cyclones, and blood-red angry slashes. When all of the pages are defaced, you carefully put the crayons away, tuck Mudball's assignment book back in her desk, and shut the lid.

When the parents arrive later in the afternoon and are asked to review their children's assignment books, Mudball's mother, Mrs. Lila Sloane actually looks embarrassed. "What's *wrong* with you?" she hisses at Mudball. Mudball just laughs.

Your parents look smug as they review your impeccably executed homework. Your father gives you a thumbs-up sign. You think maybe you should feel better, happier somehow, at this moment, but you don't. Instead, you feel as if every ugly, mean-spirited scribble is an ugly, mean-spirited secret about yourself that you will now have to keep forever.

Permanent-markered.

Non-water-soluble.

Once again, you've miscalculated the distance to the end of the lane, executed an illegal flip-turn. The flushed shame of the red flag coming down, a black DQ scrawled across your time card.

# Meta/Couch

When you go to the artist's retreat you bring along books written by each of your three lovers, all writers. You want to feel close to them, to hold their words next to you in the solitude. You imagine yourself laying down your own words alongside theirs, braiding your language into the currents of their language. For you, this feels like writerly intimacy, a kind of aesthetic sex.

It's lonely at the writer's residency. You don't call or text anyone because you can't afford international roaming. No one talks to you. You thought Canadians were supposed to be nice, but it occurs to you that maybe they don't like Americans. And why should they?

Some of it, though, is probably your own fault. After you spend all day alone in your room, writing, your focus becomes pulled so far back into your own head that by the time you wander down to the dining room you feel blinky and overlit—as if you're a pale grub who's just crawled out from under a fallen log. You feel floaty, strange, jet-lagged. The altitude makes you a little dizzy.

But still. Days pass and you feel increasingly estranged and awkward. This seems to be in direct correlation to the degree in which the surrounding scenery becomes increasingly beautiful. The rain stops, and blue-green mountains surface from behind their veils of mist like gigantic, dewy-faced brides. Clouds wobble and teeter above like excessively frosted wedding cakes. You, on the other hand, become more and more transparent—like Saran Wrap, or the Invisible Woman (pre-Malice era)—fading/melting into the scenery.

Sometimes, at mealtimes, when you get up from your table to refill your water glass, waitstaff clears your place setting and takes away your food before you're finished. One night, when you're relaxing on the roof deck after dinner, someone deadbolts the sliding patio door from the inside, leaving you locked outside on the deck. You call and call the switchboard, but no one answers. When you finally reach the switchboard, it takes security nearly an hour to come and let you back inside.

You become invisible to your lovers as well, even though their words are strong and vibrant in your head. One by one, they start to look straight through you, until they're meeting the gaze of someone else entirely.

The Ecuadoran Poet gets back together with her ex-girlfriend. They semaphore their happiness on Facebook. The Ecuadoran Poet posts that the Ex-Girlfriend Who Is Now Her Girlfriend Again memorizes entire poems by the Ecuadoran Poet, recites them back to her in multiple languages in the evenings. That's the mark of true love, fans of the Ecuadoran Poet sigh ickily into the comments section. The Ecuadoran Poet posts a picture of herself in bed with the Ex-Girlfriend Who Is Now Her Girlfriend Again in which their long, perfect, naked legs are intertwined. You feel chagrined on behalf of your not-long and not-perfect legs.

The Meta-Fictional Novelist Who May or May Not Be in the Midst of a Midlife Crisis seems to have broken things off with you as well, although he doesn't actually tell you this. Instead, he quits texting. One by one, he withdraws <3s at the end of his messages. Four <3s go to three <3s go to two <3s go to no <3s. He only emails if you email first. His replies are blandly neutral. Harried, distant. He promises to send longer emails soon, then doesn't. It reminds you of the time you rode a horse that tried to scrub you off on a fence.

Minimal creeping reveals the Meta-Fictional Novelist Who May or May Not Be in the Midst of a Midlife Crisis is likewise semaphoring newfound conjugal happiness on FB. He's saying *Yes! To the Universe!* He posts a picture of himself captioned: *Saying Yes to the Universe!* He wears a tie! With a big *Yes!* on it. The woman he's apparently saying *Yes to the Universe!* with simultaneously posts a corresponding picture of a red glass heart nestled on her pillow. It says *Yes!* A week later they get matching tattoos. The tattoos say *Yes!*

Now your only remaining lover is the Poet Who's Married to Someone Else. It's because he's married to someone else that you took the other two lovers in the first place. Because you wanted to move forward. Because you didn't want to be perpetually hostaged in the poet's bad marriage to someone else. The Poet Who's Married to Someone Else is weird and brilliant and funny and sexy and kind, but being with him is like trying to untie an infinite series of Gordian Knots. The Poet Who's Married to Someone Else makes promises like bright, extravagant runaway kites spiraling away in the wind. Of course you should know better, but you're a poet, and you like kites, too!

Maybe, in your own fashion, you've been trying to find ways to say *Yes to the Universe!* Although? For the record? You think *Saying Yes to the Universe!* is a dipshit phrase. You'd rather gouge your own eye out with a rusted spork than ever say anything that *dipshitty*.

Everything comes unbraided. You hide your lovers' books in the closet and now there's only the sound of your own voice—disconsolate, but loud and true. You think maybe it's all sort of OK but wish it weren't happening while you were alone on retreat in another country. It's the first time you've gone on an artist's retreat. You can't help but wonder if maybe you're doing it all wrong.

Now the Poet Who's Married to Someone Else keeps LIKE-ing saucy pictures of third-wave twenty-something poets *en dishabille* on FB. You can't tell if he's just being friendly or if he's articulating a newfound preference. But since he's the only one left, it makes you anxious. All the saucy-pictured third-wave twenty-something poets *en dishabille* have Tumblrs. You wonder if you should start a Tumblr. You don't feel as if you can say anything to the Poet Who's Married to Someone Else about LIKE-ing the saucy pictures of third-wave twenty-something poets because you don't want to sound creepy and insecure, and because it seems hypocritical since, strictly speaking, the Poet Who's Married to Someone Else doesn't know about the Ecuadoran Poet or the Meta-Fictional Novelist Who May or May Not Be in the Midst of a Midlife Crisis.

And *fuck* FB anyways. What used to seem like a little harmless pointing and clicking's been visually blown all out of proportion. Now each time the Poet Who's Married to Someone Else clicks LIKE, a ginormous photo of a saucy third-wave twenty-something poet *en dishabille* shows up in your feed, below a blaring notification that the Poet Who's Married to Someone Else LIKES her saucy picture. It kind of makes it hard to get perspective.

One night over Skype you tell the Poet Who's Married to Someone Else about the secretary—the one no one liked because she was mean and incompetent. The one who was fired following a small-town local scandal in which it was revealed she'd been embezzling money from her bowling league. You tell the Poet Who's Married to Someone Else about how Embezzling Secretary was a hoarder—the kind with several broken-down cars in her front yard and drawers full of grubby rubber bands. At work, it was very difficult to thread one's way to Embezzling Secretary's desk to make Xeroxing or travel reimbursement requests (tasks Embezzling Secretary would grudgingly perform with a bewildering level of incompetence and at a date so late as to be no longer useful) because her work area was walled off with old file folders, magazines, newspapers, used toner cartridges, Styrofoam, dusty Christmas ornaments, and plastic fruit. Maybe these two things—embezzling and hoarding—were all really part of the same impulse for Embezzling Secretary, you tell the Poet Who's Married to Someone Else. It was hard to say for sure.

After the Embezzling Secretary had breast-reduction surgery, a different secretary, Gossiping Secretary, came over to the Embezzling Secretary's house with obligatory post-surgery hot dish. Gossiping Secretary reported that there were two couches in Embezzling Secretary's house—one planted right in front of the other. Apparently, when the springs in the old couch were shot and Embezzling Secretary's husband started to complain that his ass hurt, Embezzling Secretary bought a new couch and they just stuck it right in front of the old couch. After that, Embezzling Secretary and her ass-hurting husband sat on the new couch, pretending like the old couch directly behind the new couch wasn't even there.

"And so here's the thing," you tell the Poet Who's Married to Someone Else over Skype: "I don't want to be that couch."

"Sweetheart, you're the farthest thing from a couch," the Poet Who's Married to Someone Else says. "I love you so much."

"I'm serious," you say. "There are way too many couches here."

"Wait," says the Poet Who's Married to Someone Else. "Is this a metaphor?" (The Poet Who's Married to Someone Else isn't *that* kind of poet.) "Which couch *don't* you want to be?"

"Neither one," you say, and now you're trying to hide on Skype that you've started to cry. "Please," you say.

"I mean it," you say.

"Don't make me be that couch."

# Other People's Therapists

It's like being a mooch, but only a little. Like when your sweetheart's going to do a laundry run, and you ask if it's all right to throw in a few pairs of underwear and maybe a couple of stockings. And your sweetheart says yes you can, and so you do, but you're *considerate* about it. The few pairs of underwear and maybe a couple of stockings stay just *that*: a few pairs of underwear and maybe a couple of stockings. You don't take *advantage*. You don't then try to also slip in a couple of T-shirts, and just this one pair of jeans, and oh, would it also be OK to maybe toss in this hoodie, too?

Only in your instance, it's not so much laundry as it is psychoanalytical insight that you're mooching.

But only a *little*.

A partial listing of sexual partners from whom you may have occasionally mooched a little bit of therapy:

(1) During the time when you're doing whatever it is you're doing with Paul Goodman, he sees a therapist he likes to refer to as Saintly Therapist Don. You feel this makes Paul Goodman sound not only like more of a bad boy than he really is, but also significantly much more forthcoming than he really is. The acronym for Saintly

Therapist Don (which you perhaps point out a bit too gleefully to Paul Goodman) is, of course, STD, which makes Paul Goodman frown. Paul Goodman apparently likes to talk to STD at length about The Silo—a construct you've never been quite able to get an exact conceptual grip on. The Silo seems to be a metaphor for boundaries, but still … so much remains unclear! For example, is it a *nuclear* Silo, or a *grain* silo? A differentiation that seems crucial, yes? And is The Silo meant to keep busybodies and unwelcome intruders out—possibly indicating that Paul Goodman has bad boundaries, is maybe even somewhat codependent? Or is The Silo some sort of cloistered form of self-imprisonment from which Paul Goodman needs coaxing out of? In other words, who's Paul Goodman protecting? Himself, or others? Or does he imagine, bad-boyishly, that he's protecting *others*, when he's really protecting *himself*?

Paul Goodman confesses that he once spent most of a session with STD worrying about (transference? codependency?) whether or not STD noticed and liked Paul Goodman's new shoes.

The thing STD once told Paul Goodman, though, that you think is brilliant, is that the way people behave toward you ultimately doesn't reveal things about *you*, but rather it reveals things about *them*.

(2) When you were having an affair with Cale, thereby flinging him headlong into his "tale of woe," as he likes to refer to your time together (which you think is rather unnecessarily melodramatic), he immediately—despite

never having been in therapy before—begins seeing two therapists: one a male psychiatrist, who also manages his meds, and the other a female counselor, who Cale lies to. These are the things Cale lies to his counselor about: (a) the fact that he still continues to phone and email you, despite having promised his wife, Mariah, that he would stop phoning and emailing you; and (b) the fact that he's signed a lease on a studio sublet (which he also hasn't told Mariah about), which he never actually moves into, but sometimes visits in the afternoons. When you ask what he does in the afternoons there, in his secret sublet, he says he usually just takes a nap.

Cale's psychiatrist, to whom he *hasn't* been lying, apparently likes to refer to you as "The [Your Name Here] Syndrome." When you tell Paul Goodman about this, he seems impressed.

"Wow, you've got a whole syndrome named after you?" he says. "I wish somebody's therapist would name a syndrome after *me*."

At which point you suggest that Paul Goodman might like to go back inside his Silo.

Cale's psychiatrist frequently proffers the idea that "The [Your Name Here] Syndrome" is a surface manifestation of Cale's depression, and will "resolve itself" with the right combination of meds and talk therapy, which makes you feel like a *pathology*.

That said, Cale's marriage *does* begin to seem depressing to you. But more so for Mariah, his estranged wife, than for Cale. You soon begin to find all of his daytime solipsistic hand-wringing (before going home to matter-of-factly eat a dinner Mariah's *prepared* for him, then to sleep in sheets and pajamas Mariah's *washed* for him) *intensely* irritating.

And so when he begins to dump irrational flaming bricks of shit at your doorstep for decades-long issues he has with Mariah, but has never actually bothered to *talk to Mariah about*, well … it's baffling because he's a brilliant man, but mostly it's *profoundly* off-putting. It's never really occurred to you before that there could be such a *sharp* bifurcation between intellectual and emotional brilliance.

This is the amazing thing, though, that stays with you from Cale's recounting of his therapy sessions: Apparently, during one of the sessions with the female counselor that he lies to, in which Cale was trying to understand his father's abusively irrational behavior following his mother's death, Cale's counselor interrupts him to ask, "Why are you trying to make sense of *crazy*?"

(3) When you first meet The Beloved, he's seeing a cognitive behavioralist, which seems to mean she doesn't believe in discussing concrete coping strategies or in applying particular diagnoses. You find this somewhat troubling since, to your mind, engaging with The Beloved during this time period is a bit like trying to grasp a soybean glazed in sesame oil with a pair of plastic chopsticks. But maybe this is just sour grapes on your part? Because when The Beloved's therapist (who you and The Beloved nickname DoctorKathyAcker [all one word]) tells The Beloved, shortly before he

meets you, that his marriage isn't an *actual* marriage—encouraging him to conceptualize, acknowledge, and verbally describe to himself and others the ways in which his marriage is completely nonfunctional, estranged, and *separate*—you're pretty sure she doesn't mean for the Beloved to use "separat*ed*" as an actual descriptor by which to semaphore his marital status to potential romantic partners.

But that's all water under the bridge now. Plus, later on, DoctorKathyAcker (all one word) says something to The Beloved, in reference to his marriage, that you feel has possibly saved your life. Maybe this sounds hyperbolic, but no … it's true. You think this thing that DoctorKathyAcker (all one word) says to The Beloved has, in fact, saved your life. What she says to The Beloved is this: *How does the lobster know it's in boiling water if it's being told it's relaxing in a cool and soothing bath?*

(As an aside, The Beloved's current meds psychiatrist, Dr. Ranganathan, seems to be a bit senile—inconsistent with dosages, shifty with her meds cocktails, and forgetful about calling in prescriptions. She apparently repeatedly asks The Beloved the same diagnostic questions during each monthly visit, such as: "If you were inside a burning building, what would you do?")

So. What *would* you do, if you were inside a burning building?

People ask about your therapist, then seem surprised to learn you aren't seeing one. How do you explain, without coming across as flippant, that you can't actually bring yourself to *do* therapists, that you find therapists *triggering*?

How to express the betrayal of being eight years old, sitting in the psychiatrist's office, and having to explain—yet again—what the boy who lives across the street has done to you? The shame of having to say—yet again—the words out loud. You've begged your parents—who say what happened to you was your fault because you were *stupid*—to tell you a biologically accurate, adult word for your genitalia so you won't have to say the baby word in front of the psychiatrist, but they don't seem to understand, or empathize with, what the enormity of this indignity feels like for you.

And in the end, after having to confess the particular ways in which the boy across the street molested you, after having to bring yourself to use the baby word, the psychiatrist says that you're obviously a very bright girl, but are clearly mistaken about what was done to you and by whom. For years, you feel that if you hadn't had to use the baby word, or if you'd only found a way to present yourself as smarter, as better, as somehow more *believable*, the psychiatrist (who, it seems, is asked by the parents of the boy across the street to "judge" the case of your having been molested by their son), would have taken your side. But how this psychiatrist chose to respond to you was never about *you*. Her actions were always about *her*. Thanks to Paul Goodman, you know this now.

Because here's the thing: The boy across the street's father is a medical doctor, and the psychiatrist is a colleague of his. Afterwards, your parents complain bitterly that the psychiatrist is "in cahoots"—those are the words they use, "in cahoots"—with the parents of the boy across the street. Even as a child, you wonder why your parents would agree to send you not to your *own* psychiatrist, but to one who so clearly already belongs to the boy across the street? Your parents say pressing charges against the boy who lives across the street is futile, and instead, they forbid you to tell anyone what happened because now you are "damaged goods."

Soon after, you begin to deal with the anxiety of living across the street from the boy who lives across the street by cutting. Your parents punish you severely for cutting: enraged "wallopings" with wooden paint paddles in the basement, your father so angry he sometimes breaks the paddles when he hits you with them. Your parents threaten to send you to see a counselor, as if *this* is the ultimate shame, or punishment. They infer that seeing a counselor means they will no longer be able to protect the secret of how monstrous you've truly become.

At the same time, your parents repeatedly insist no one will ever tell you "the truth" about yourself but them. According to your parents, *everyone* (your teachers, their neighbors, your classmates) is saying bad things about you, laughing at you behind your back. Your parents say the only people you can trust are your parents, that you can't believe anyone else, that you know this is true because you can "trust them" to tell you all the bad things about yourself. The list of bad things is very,

very long—all of these shameful secrets about you your parents are apparently protecting by only *threatening* to send you to see a therapist. And yet, paradoxically, these are also the bad things everyone is always/already saying behind your back? Whenever you begin to get tangled up with these memories in this particular way, this is when you channel Cale's therapist and ask yourself: *Why do you keep trying to make sense of crazy?*

*How does the lobster know it's in boiling water if it's being told it's relaxing in a cool and soothing bath?*

You're nine years old and you've left your favorite doll lying down in her baby carriage too long and now the curls on the back of her head are flattened down, and you can see pink plastic through her matted nylon hair. She is *ruined*. You find her unspeakably *loathsome*.

You steal one of your father's paint paddles and beat her in the attic with it.

You make her sit naked in the corner with her face to the wall.

Your doll won't tell on you.

You tell her she's ugly, she jiggles her foot, she always has a stupid-looking expression on her face, she's lazy, her neck isn't long enough, she hits wrong notes when she plays the piano, she puts inside-out socks in the laundry basket, she's a *self-mutilator*, and everything that happens to her is her own fault.

"No one will love you the way I will," you tell your doll.

The doll stares at you quietly with the stupid-looking expression on her face. Of course, she doesn't talk back.

Because this doll?

Your doll?

She won't tell.

She will *never ever tell.*

# O, Canada!

It's the summer the Okanagan's on fire, and everything's obscured by smoke, including the doomed nature of fucking your stoner Canadian girlfriend from grad school. Even though it's an entire province away, the smoke creates a hazy gray cloud cover most days, fogging up the intensely honeyed summer sunlight. It lends an air of solemnity, you feel, to the national parks and interpretive centers you visit with Jorunn—your friend from grad school who now teaches piano in Lethbridge. You go to see Head Smashed In Buffalo Jump—where the Pigan routed migrating herds of buffalo through a series of cairns until they stampeded over a sharp rocky cliff. And you drive to Frank Slide in the Crowsnest Pass—where the entire coal-mining town of Frank was suddenly buried in rubble during the night Turtle Mountain (a mountain that, according to indigenous oral history, was rumored to *move*) unexpectedly avalanched.

Perhaps you should have more carefully heeded the Okanagan on fire, the ghosts and seared afterimages of buffalo and mountains tumbling down through the smoky haze, as *portents* of sorts?

In fact, Jorunn's weed dealer, Geoffrey, doesn't seem to have any difficulty stating the obvious. "You live over 1,000 miles apart in different *countries*," he cheerfully says to you one night while Jorunn's using the washroom. "You know it's never going to actually *work*, right?"

But then again, Geoffrey's always had a bit of a soft spot for you. An agoraphobe, Geoffrey (in addition to selling pot) runs an eBay listing business out of his parents' basement. Basically, people pick up stuff at garage sales, estate sales, and thrifts, then bring it to Geoffrey to sell on eBay. He knows you love insects, so he always sets aside insect mounts and other insect-related finds for you.

Geoffrey has a disturbingly huge bull mastiff named Mycroft. When you first meet Mycroft, Geoffrey tells you it's important to maintain direct eye contact with the enormous dog. Which you do, and you and Mycroft soon become very good friends, although you notice that whenever you wear your hair down, Mycroft always stares at you a bit too intently and gets a hard-on, which you find disconcerting.

Nonetheless, you're hopelessly captivated. Maybe it's the stunning thrust of the Canadian Rockies. They remind you of the American Rockies, where you grew up, but seem even *more* chest-clenchingly beautiful, if that's at all possible. (Is it because *these* Rockies come without the ugly dramas of your childhood home?) Maybe it's the humanely progressive health care system, the funny comedy shows on the CBC (*The Red Green Show, This Hour Has 22 Minutes*), or the environmentally responsible recycling policies. Or maybe it's Jorunn's hilarious sense of humor, her matter-of-fact, strapping *Norwegian*-ness.

You're very charmed by the way she uses "eh" as a verbal pause and pronounces "about" *aboot* and "progress" *proh-gress*.

In this mania-inducing summer light, which lasts (even with the haze of smoke from the Okanagan being on fire) until well past 10 p.m., the ghosts of tumbling buffalo and avalanching mountain slides seem—from a certain, hopeful angle—like metaphors for lovers leaping, or the inevitability of waterfalls. Jorunn invites you to stay the whole summer—after all, you can write anywhere, right?—and soon, you've met all her friends and most of her family. You and Jorunn start joking around a lot about getting married in Canada, where it's recently become legal, and then you'd have dual citizenship, eh?

Which isn't to say there aren't any red flags. You notice, for example, that Jorunn can't even go to the grocery store without packing a one-hitter in the car. And one morning she leaves her journal open in the exact spot where you always sit to have your morning coffee, making it all but impossible to notice that she's written, about you, in *shoutycaps*: DO I REALLY WANT TO TAKE ON SOMEONE WHO HAS TO TAKE MEDS FOR OCD?!?!

But still, it's as if you've been hypnotized by the beautiful white cycling of giant windmills turning and turning on their windmill farms at the base of the Rockies across vast, riffling yellow fields of canola flowers. And so you keep on existing in this hazy Canadian dream, and it isn't until you drive back down to the States at the end of the summer that things come unraveled.

At first it's a growing tension in the car. Jorunn's on her period, her cramps are bad, and she asks you to drive. "I wouldn't have cramps if I could get high," she mutters pointedly before going to sleep for most of the twenty-four-hour drive, as if her cramps are all *your* fault.

It's true, you refused to cross the border with marijuana in the car. Jorunn hasn't been down to the States since 9/11. She seems to think you're exaggerating when you describe what happened when you tried to re-enter with just a birth certificate after a literature conference in Toronto—how you were forced to recite the Pledge of Allegiance and the words to "The Star Spangled Banner" at the airport, and it was a 5:45 a.m. flight and you were horridly *uncaffeinated* and hard-pressed to recite even your own *name*. How you couldn't remember all the lines and for a moment things looked sketchy, as if they might not let you back in. As it is, when you end up crossing, the U.S. Border Patrol searches Jorunn's car and confiscates the fruit packed in her cooler, which just pisses her off even more. When she wakes up, she nags and backseat drives: too slow, too fast, why'd you stop for gas in a place so far off the interstate?

Then when you finally arrive, she's rude to your friends, who've been eager to meet her. She keeps telling everyone, including your colleagues, that you've *always* been "spinny"—which is apparently Canadian-ese for *ditzy*. When you tactfully express polite interest in a project suggested by your acting chair, she sing-songs "You're *ly-ing*," while he's still within earshot.

On a day trip to Sioux Falls, a skinny teenager rolls down his window and calls you "faggots" as you're pulling out of the parking lot of the Sertoma Butterfly House. He's a truck-driving cliché in a corn seed cap with a bulging lump of chew in his lower lip.

"Excuse me?" you say, rolling down your window.

"Faggots," he says. "Fucking *faggots*. With a fucking faggot *sticker* on your car!"

Before you have a chance to reply, Jorunn leans across you and yells, "I'm going to kick your fucking ass!" then starts charging out of the passenger side of your car. You have to restrain her by the collar of her shirt. The boy gives you the finger and pulls out of the parking lot, tires squealing.

"What, you're going to beat up a *teenager*?" you ask Jorunn.

"I tell you what," she says, "it's a *really* good thing I love you."

And you have to wonder to yourself: *Is it? Is it* really *a good thing?*

Why haven't you noticed this flattening behind the eyes before, the slight darkening of the pupils? It reminds you of your mother, in that eye-of-the-tornado instant before she'd whirlwind into one of her inexplicable borderline rages. Have you not been paying enough attention? Hypervigilance is your middle name, though, so this doesn't seem likely. Is it because Jorunn's on edge and out of her comfort zone? Or is it because you don't have any idea who Jorunn really *is* anymore when she's not high?

On your fifth or sixth night back in the States, you're sick with stomach flu, or maybe it's food poisoning, you're not sure, and Jorunn wants to have sex, but you don't. She doesn't want to take no for an answer, and you have to physically shove her away from you. She pulls down her pants and begins masturbating—loudly, grotesquely, in your bed. You go into your bathroom, where you slam and lock the door. You end up cutting yourself. The next morning, when she sees the bandaged evidence of the cuts, she says, "Why don't you just put a fucking gun to your head?" And that's when you tell her to leave.

How many years do we have to serve time in relationships with trickster versions of our raging borderline mothers, our hair-trigger-temper fathers, our narcissistic and passive aggressive palimpsestic loves?

How many days/weeks/months does it take to realize that we're *still*, despite our best efforts, serving time in relationships with trickster versions of our raging borderline mothers, our hair-trigger-temper fathers, our narcissistic and passive-aggressive palimpsestic loves?

How many lifetimes do we have to live before we stop secretly believing we somehow *deserve* to serve time in relationships with trickster versions of our raging borderline mothers, our hair-trigger-temper fathers, our narcissistic and passive-aggressive palimpsestic loves?

☾

You go No Contact, and after several months of flowers, unanswered phone calls and emails, Jorunn sends you a handwritten letter, in which she accuses you of discarding her *like yesterday's newspaper*. She implies she's been feeling suicidal. She threatens to drive down and make you *deal* with her, face-to-face. You think of Elizabeth Bishop's lover, Lota, who unexpectedly arrived in the United States following their breakup in Brazil, and how Lota then killed herself that first night in Elizabeth Bishop's New York City bathroom.

But then you also think of how orphaned, peripatetic Bishop—torn away as a child from her Canadian motherland in Nova Scotia—was always searching for family, for home. You think of how Lota offered Bishop a place to stay, and write, and how—before it became really, really *bad*—it was good.

You think of the smell of sweetgrass and sage, the glacier-carved swells of coulees, and the ghost towns, the abandoned collieries, winding up switchback after switchback all the way up into the Crowsnest Pass, and how, at least for one impossibly bright summer, this felt like *home* to you. Crowned by a *family* of mountains—the Seven Sisters, jutting into cloud-dolloped sky with their dizzying and otherworldly beauty.

And then the bison spilling off the rock cliff. And then the entire face of a mountain sliding off, destroying a whole town, and O, Canada, *O, Canada!*

# The Deer Who Killed the Man

It was after losing the tobacco case, which had consumed nearly a decade of his professional and personal life, that he began to experience an uneasy sense of something crucial having been taken away from him, although he couldn't actually identify exactly *what* that something was. But it bothered him. Even though, despite the loss, he was named a partner in the international corporate law firm where he worked, he still felt as if he'd been, through some sort of cosmic sleight of hand, somehow *diminished*, and nothing—not even the new house, or the new boat for their vacation home on Lake Erie, or the ill-advised and hideously clichéd affair with Gwenn, one of the paralegals from the Ohio Clerk of Courts, or the tediously numerous rounds of golf—did anything to alleviate this sense of diminishment.

One night, after a celebratory round of late-night cigars and single-malt scotch, he confessed this sense of malaise to one of the senior partners, who—with the grandiosity of the extremely privileged—advised him to *expand his horizons*. This conversation stuck with him, because what he'd been feeling had been, in fact, a kind of *hemmed-in-ness*. He liked the sound of the word, *horizons*, particularly in conjunction with *expansiveness*. It made him think, with a certain sense of nostalgia, of how he'd felt in prep school reading Hemingway's Nick Adams stories. He decided that, even though he'd never really been an *outdoorsy* person, that he wanted to reclaim his sense of well-being through being in *the great outdoors*. This was actually the phrase he used to himself inside his own head: *the great outdoors*. He began to entertain fantasies of himself with a rifle—scouting, tracking, and victoriously shooting a large-antlered buck. And just like that, he decided to take up deer hunting.

From then on, the image of taking down a deer consumed all of his thoughts and all of his non-billable hours, and he meticulously prepared, as if litigating a court case in which he represented the plaintiff and the deer was the defendant.

*Complaint:*

He filed for a deer hunting license at Stinks Bait, Tackle & Convenience Store. Although he could have easily gone through the state Department of Wildlife website and purchased a license online, he decided he preferred the *gravitas* of applying for the license at a local bait-and-tackle. And so he asked his secretary to block off his calendar so that he could leave work early one afternoon, and he drove his Mercedes-Benz GLS SUV down to Stinks, feeling rich with ceremony.

At Stinks, the regular customers side-eyed him in his navy Brooks Brothers suit and lavender power tie, but he ignored them. Instead, he jingled his change and confidently strolled past the aisles of glittering lures and aluminum signage pointing toward a grimy refrigerator full of live bait to the counter in the back and told the owner—an older man with Scotch-taped half-specs sliding down toward the bottom of a hawk nose—that he'd come to purchase a deer-hunting license.

*Discovery:*

"I would get it if your father used to take you hunting and this were some sort of a nostalgia thing," his wife said to him one evening, after he returned from lessons at the shooting range with Brandon, a former NCAA rifle champion for the Ohio Valley Conference. "But this sudden obsession of yours seems, I don't know, totally *random*. Plus, you know how I feel about having a gun in the house with the kids."

"What? It's a wholesome, American pastime," he reassured his wife, slipping into the easy braggadocio of the courtroom. "Plus, when Nick's older, I can take him hunting with me. It'll be, like, an *heirloom hobby*. Father-son bonding," he added. "You're always complaining that I spend too much time at the office and not enough time with the kids."

His wife frowned. "Don't badger," she said warningly, referring to his penchant for handling conversations with her as if she were a troublesome litigant—a point that had been circled around with much frequency during the siege of couples counseling they attended post-Gwenn. "Also, I don't understand why you can't start with something smaller. How about a turkey, for example? Thanksgiving's coming."

"Turkeys are for pussies," he said.

She shook her head. "Whatever. But you're not bringing a dead deer into this house. That's where I put my foot down."

He grinned, pressing his advantage into a favorable ruling. "I'll take it to a processing plant. We'll have a freezer full of venison sausage."

Three weeks later, he successfully passed his hunter certification test.

*Interrogatories:*

He studied the semiotics of deer, learned to search for deer antler rubbings on mature trees, signifying the territorial markings of a dominant buck. He mastered how to identify a deer scrape—an area cleared by a pawing hoof, particularly along the edges of woods and fields—and to check the scrape for fresh urine or fecal markings. He became skilled in observing twig licking as social communication, and learned that an ideal spot to place a blind was near a twig-licking site.

*Depositions:*

He drove to the Cabela's in Avon and purchased a host of tools for deer calling: an EZ Doe Bleat Plus Call that created "realistic fawn-in-distress" bleats to lure in protective does and attract curious bucks; a Nemesis Grunt Call which simulated sounds made during rutting, guaranteed to produce "lifelike midtone deep grunts and roars that bring in the big bucks"; a Slam Talker Deer Grunt Call, which replicated the characteristic snort/

wheeze sound made by bucks when trying to intimidate and "rile up other bucks"; as well as an authentic pair of Rattling Antlers to "draw the big boys in close."

*Voir Dire:*

Because he had a friend whose brother-in-law swore to the efficacy of this strategy, he packed his newly purchased hunting clothes and his camouflage hat in leaves so he wouldn't smell strange to the deer. His goal was to render himself completely "invisible" to the deer. He also packed a camera, to document the hunt, and his rosary beads, too, for good luck.

*Evidence:*

Three days in the deer blind, and there was nothing.

He bleated, grunted, roared, rattled, and snort-wheezed, and still, there was nothing.

He tried waiting silently and there was nothing.

At one point, he heard a sudden rustling in the leaves. Becoming overly excited, he blindly fired off his rifle in the direction of the noise. The rustling stopped. Clambering out of the blind to investigate, he found a small rabbit with its head blown off. The rifle, needless to say, was excessive.

A bit unnerved, flustered, and unsure of what to do, he left the remains of the rabbit alone, and returned to the deer blind, where he took out his rosary beads and began to finger them.

That's when the hunt took a strange turn. A flock of turkeys moved into the clearing in front of his blind—cutting and bobbing and yelping. Pausing at the sight of the headless rabbit, they slowly began to circle it. Twenty-three turkeys—he counted them—quietly walking around and around and around the dead rabbit in single file. Almost entirely silent, with the exception of the occasional cluck or purr.

He waited for the turkeys to leave, his anxiety mounting, but around they went, on and on. After a half hour of this, he couldn't stand it any longer, and so he leaped out of the blind, shouting, and waving his arms. He fired his rifle in the air. The turkeys scattered, and even though he'd planned to stay at least another night, and even though the smell of snow was in the air, he hastily broke down his camp, packed it all back out to his car, and began the five-hour drive home.

*Closing:*

Two hours later, on a rural Ohio road, with snow filtering down like television static, the man, whose goal was to "become invisible to the deer" did indeed become invisible to a deer, when one startled from the woods and leaped in front of his Mercedes.

The impact was terrible, and he rested dazed for several long moments, cheek against the deployed airbag, hiss of the radiator exhaling a plume of steam into the frozen air. The front of the car was crumpled. Totaled, he thought to himself.

In the headlights, the man could see the prone body of the deer, a large buck—the spitting image of his dream buck, even—on the road. But then after another minute or so, the buck twitched, then rose up on quavering legs and shook itself off, before trotting back off into the woods on the other side of the road.

The man blinked. He wondered if he could smell gasoline. Clumsily, he tore off his seatbelt, and jumped out of the drivers' side door. He fell, and scrabbled over to the side of the road, where he sat in the several inches of accumulated snow, panting.

When he gathered his wits a little more, realizing the car wasn't about to explode, he got up and brushed off the snow, and made his way back to the vehicle, feeling strangely chagrined. He discovered his crushed cell phone in the snow outside the open driver's side door. He must have stepped on it with his steel-toed hunting boot during his hasty exit. Cursing, he located the emergency flares from the trunk and set them up around the car, then waited for help to come by.

*Verdict:*

The car wouldn't even turn over, and the snow kept falling. Soon, the man could no longer feel his fingers or his toes. His nose and ears burned with a searing, icy pain.

It occurred to him that for all of his preparation—his complicated rituals, strategies, gadgets to create a ruse in which to ultimately fool his prey—the deer was the one who had somehow managed to prevail.

The barometer continued to plummet, and he realized that his situation was become increasingly dire. He shivered in his wrecked car, fighting off the urge to sleep.

He wondered, in a kind of loopy hysteria, if it was too late to settle with the deer for losing a couple of extremities—a few fingers or toes? maybe the edges of his ears?—to frostbite.

Before he nodded off, he thought about the scourge of turkeys, and imagined them, silently circling his demolished car. Around and around. Around and around. Around and—

# Sundowning, with Fat Juice

You try to make sure and leave the assisted living center before 7 p.m.; otherwise your Japanese mother has a mood crash and initiates a hostile litany of grievances against your stroke-addled father, which—even though she occasionally makes a good point—is still difficult for you to stomach.

Nonetheless, you sometimes don't manage to make it out in time, and once she starts in, it becomes difficult to extricate yourself. As soon as your mother sighs loudly and asks, "Why I have to live such horrible life?" you know you've waited too long.

You've been spending the entirety of your summer off from teaching college sleeping on a foam pad on your parents' living room floor, despite your spinal stenosis, as you painstakingly attempt to sift through the Stage 4 hoarding situation at their house. One of the epicenters of hoarding is in your childhood bedroom, which your father has transformed into a classic hamster's nest: old bills dating back to the 1970s mixed in with junk mail mixed in with sensitive financial and legal documents mixed in with cracked eight-track tapes mixed in with books and newspapers mixed in with gun magazines mixed in with empty prescription bottles mixed in with stale chocolate mixed in with used urinary pads mixed in with discount-bin videocassette tapes mixed in with pamphlets for injectable erectile dysfunction meds—all stuffed into precariously stacked and collapsing cardboard flats of Ramen noodle containers.

It's upsetting and disturbing, and you feel like an archaeologist searching for the K-Pg boundary demarcating the Cretaceous-Paleogene mass extinction event, which ended the reign of the dinosaurs. Not to mention you've already discovered five *loaded* handguns haphazardly hidden throughout the room. Sometimes, you consider bringing up the presence of the loaded handguns with your parents when you join them for dinner at their assisted living center, but afterwards, they invariably begin fighting about the Fat Juice, which is what your Japanese mother calls the vanilla Ensure they both like. Back in their apartment after dinner, your father will usually suggest that everyone have a cold drink, which is his way of saying that he wants a Fat Juice.

"No!" your mother tells him. "You drinking my Fat Juice like *water*! So *expensive*! And then you going to go to bathroom on new mattress your daughter *bought* for us."

"It's the only kind of cold drink that's any *good*," your father says, plaintively.

"Let him have a Fat Juice," you say, since you've been bankrolling the Fat Juice supply. "I'm happy to buy you both as much Fat Juice as you want."

"You shut *up*," your mother says to you. "Don't try stick your nose in our business." She opens the refrigerator and after carefully eyeing the contents, eventually decides to offer a half-empty, flat diet ginger ale to your father. "Here, you finish this first," she says.

"I don't *like* that!" your father yells.

"Then you don't get cold drink!" your mother yells back.

"*Good*!" your father yells. He rolls his wheelchair into the bedroom and stares out the window.

"Your father, he drinking up *all* my Fat Juice," your mother says to you, sotto voce. "And then last night, do you know what happen? I been waiting all day to drink my Fat Juice, and he drinking drinking *glub glub glub* three or four! But I been saving mine until end of day to enjoy, and then I ask him if he want half of my Fat Juice, and you know what he say? He say no, he don't *want* any. What kind of *stink person* going to act that way?"

You wait until your mother has to go to the bathroom, then you quietly slip your father a Fat Juice and wheel him back into the living room.

In point of fact, your mother's life is not—by any reasonable standard—horrible at all. While you understand that she misses her house, her cycle of habits that have the deep-rootedness of an ingrown toenail, she's eighty-seven years old, frail, and suffering from significant memory issues. By comparison, the assisted living center you've moved her into with your father is clean, sanitary, devoid of hoarding issues, comfortable, safe, and professionally staffed. Still, you feel *gutted* every time she raises the question: "Why I have to live such horrible life?" But maybe that's the point. Every time she asks, "Why I have to live such horrible life?" you think of the mob show, *The Sopranos*, and Livia Soprano, Tony Soprano's terrifying mother. You think of Dr. Jennifer Melfi, Tony's therapist, who tells the guilt-ridden Tony that the assisted living center where he's moved his mother is "a beautiful facility. It's more like a hotel at Cap d'Antibes." To which Tony says, "Yeah. But to her it's a nursing home." You realize it's grossly unfair to make comparisons, but still, you can't help but sometimes think of women who were or are around the same age as your mother: Yuri Kochiyama, Ruth Asawa, Aiko Herzig-Yoshinaga, Yayoi Kusama, Yoko Ono.

"Stupid, stupid, stupid!" your mother complains. "Why I decide to leave Japan to be with *this one*?" She jerks her chin in the general direction of your father's wheelchair. "If I stay Japan, I have family who take *care* of me." This is the point where you're tempted to remind her that she does have family—that *you're* her family—and that you *have* been taking care of her, but you've learned it's futile to try and contradict the veracity of these monologues.

"And *this guy* say he only going to live for maybe one or two years. Then what's going to happen to me? I all alone. What I supposed to do? Get job as *waitress*?"

"Mom," you say, "I promise that whatever happens, you're going to be well taken care of. You don't have to worry."

"But I *do* worry!" your mother says indignantly.

"I know you do," you say. "But what I'm trying to tell you is you don't *need* to. Please don't worry."

"How I can *trust* you?" asks your mother. "You always get to go here and there, and spending money like a Rockefeller! So why your opinion matter to me? And easy for you to talk. You have job, so somebody give you money every month. Somebody give you money so you go wherever you want. You know where *I* get to go?"

Assuming it's a rhetorical question, you don't answer. It's always interesting to you how, in your mother's eyes, the labor behind money is magically erased, as if it simply doesn't exist. For your mother, money isn't something that's *earned*, it's something that's *given*, and—despite the generous monthly allowance that your father gave to her, despite the fat envelopes of cash he presented to her on birthdays and holidays, despite the fact that all of their accounts and property listed both of them as joint owners—your mother's always in a state of furious certainty that whatever amount of money she's been given isn't *enough*. And it's not that you wish to erase the reality of domestic labor, or the fact that your mother clearly suffers from an undiagnosed mental illness your father was either unable or unwilling to admit or address, although you *know* he knows because he brought it up with you once in private, later on in his life. But the truth of the matter is that your mother was, at best, a highly lackadaisical housekeeper, and that the domestic caretaking she *did* provide was served up with so much hostility, resentment, and micromanagement that it always felt like having to submit to an unpleasant course of emotional blackmail. You think of your mother sleeping in every morning, then leafing through Japanese fashion magazines in bed. You think of her long afternoons spent watching soap operas and game shows. You understand that her days might have been marked by boredom, and irritation, certainly, but they were also filled with a kind of comparative ease.

"*Hey*!" your mother demands, louder. "Where *I* get to go?"

"Where?" you ask, even though you already know the answer.

"Nowhere!" says your mother. "*This guy*, he take me *nowhere*! Only selfish places *he* want to go! Even poor Chinese students, who want to come school here in United States, they go to New York City. Or they go see beautiful waterfall in Canada where people go for honeymoon. What I see? *Nothing*!"

"What's that you see?" asks your father, who's woken up after nodding off in his wheelchair, not seeming to realize that he's lined up in your mother's sights.

"I say you take me to see *nothing*!" your mother yells at him.

"Oh," says your father.

"See?" your mother says to you. "He not have anything to say. Can't defend. But then in middle of night when he wet his pants, then he want use me for help, and I all pulling pulling *pulling* try to take his pants off, and my back hurt so much, and such horrible *stink*!" Your mother seems to have no sense of, or compassion for, your father's current physical and verbal challenges.

"Mom, we talked about this," you say. "Press the button and ask for help. You shouldn't be trying to assist him in the bathroom. Let someone who's trained to do that help."

"How I can push button and ask for help in middle of night when he pushing button all day long as much as he wants?"

"Push the button," you say. "The night staff is here to help you at night. That's what you're paying for."

"I don't know about that," your mother says dubiously. "Anyway, we can't afford to stay here, such crazy expensive place. But *this guy*, he mess up and get kick out of *other place* because he *troublemaker* and complain about take *shower*! In Japan I take bath every day, but *this guy*, he such *stink* person!"

"He didn't get kicked out of the nursing home," you say. "He finished rehab. Remember? We all decided that since he can't live at home any longer, the two of you would live together here." In truth, your mother is also no longer capable of living independently, but that's not an argument you wish to broach with her.

"Why *I* have to live here, when he the one mess up and get kick out of *other* place?" Your mother steamrolls ahead. "Why I have to live such no-good place when all my things at home? Just to push *this guy* around in cart and clean up his stink pants?"

Later, you will wonder why you don't try harder to stand up for your father, although you know that when your mother is in the midst of one of her rages, rational arguments or interventions are impossible. But you also wonder why your father never stood up for you when *you* were the subject of your mother's vitriol for so many years. After all, he was an adult, and you were only a child. It makes you feel queasy when you realize your mother seems to target whomever is the most vulnerable member of the family.

"You're right," says your father, in one of his unexpected flickers of lucidity. "I'm sorry. I shouldn't be asking you to help me with that."

"Please remember to push the button, OK?" you say to your father, even though you know he won't remember. "She's not strong enough to assist you, and I'm worried she might hurt herself."

"Hello, hurt herself!" says your mother indignantly. "I been doing every night, three or four or five times, on and on! And *this guy*, he treat me worse than maid, and what he give me on Valentine's Day? *Nothing*!"

You think sadly of the gushy Valentine's Day cards, as well as the birthday and Christmas cards, you've found squirrelled away in strange places in the house from your usually undemonstrative father, bulging with $100 bills, and which your mother apparently insisted on stoically hoarding against inevitable financial ruin.

"You know what?" asks your mother, switching over to a more philosophical tone. "You know Black people, who come over to this country early time, and they get sold and work as maids?"

"Do you mean as *enslaved people*?" you ask, incredulously.

"I have it *worse* than those Black people," your mother says. "At least they got *paid*."

"Mom, *please stop*!" you say. "They were *kidnapped*, subject to an ocean crossing in *unspeakable conditions*, sold on the auction block, tortured, and forced into *brutal manual labor*. And no, for the record, they did *not* get paid!"

"You shut *up*!" says your mother. "What complete naïve you are. You don't know anything about how the world works. Such stupid." Then she turns on my father. "What *you* have to say? Thanks to you, I have it *much worse* than Black people!"

"Well, if you want to get rid of me, then I guess you can do that," says your father, who has become agitated, and is now having trouble catching his breath.

"Yes, let's get divorce. I can go live in my house again and you can stay here! I going to marry handsome millionaire!" says my mother. "But who cares? You only going to live for one or two years more anyways."

Your father disgustedly rolls his wheelchair into the bedroom.

"See?" your mother says to you, conspiratorially. "He don't have good answer."

Your mother's dark, anxious keening—manipulative, narcissistic, and delusional—never fails to slice like a hot knife through butter. It hurts you to think that perhaps she's enacting, with your father, the ultimate, final tarantella of "I hate you/don't leave me."

☾

This all happens before your father falls in the bathroom on New Year's Day at the assisted living center and dies, within hours, from a cerebral hemorrhage. You will drive all night to come take care of things, and the first thing your mother will say to you when you see her is, "I have to tell you secret. Your father, he such *stink*! He *snitch* all my money and then you know what?"

"What?" you'll ask, dumbfounded.

"He give away all my money to his *girlfriend*! But first he take several of his girlfriends out to lunch at nice restaurant downtown! Over sixty years marry and he *never* take me to nice restaurant downtown!"

And even though you'll gently try to explain the wild *unlikelihood* of your frail, wheelchair-using father *snitching* all of her money and Lothario-ing it up at the assisted living center, your mother will only become more agitated and angry. And so you'll end up reminding her that your father was suffering from "head trouble," which is your mother's term for dementia.

"That's right, he kuru-kuru-pa," your mother will say, circling her index finger around her ear. "All the time he fighting and screaming. Neighbors going to listen, then tell everyone we fighting and screaming all the time. Still," she'll add wistfully, "even though such *stink*, I miss him."

This happens before you take your mother to the funeral home to visit your father's body one last time. On the car ride there, your mother will suddenly exclaim, "I so mad about your father for being such *stink* I maybe going to *thwack* him when I see him!" But then she'll admit, a bit more quietly, "I'm scared to see him."

"I know," you'll agree. "Me, too."

"After this, I never going to see your father again," your mother will say. "After today, they going to cook him, and he only going to be flour."

Later on, after dinner, your mother will ask you, "What do you think your father doing now?"

"I don't know," you'll say. "What do *you* think he's doing?"

"I think he probably lying by himself in the dark somewhere," she'll say.

This is before your mother, with her penchant for brilliant non sequiturs, unexpectedly blurts out one night, "Your father die and we just leftovers."

You won't know what to say to her in response.

"Don't you think so?" she'll insist.

You'll shrug, because you don't want to be a leftover, and you don't want your mother to think she's a leftover, either, even if it feels a little bit true.

She'll say it to you once again. "We just leftovers."

All of this happens before the death certificate finally arrives and you learn that your father was lying on the floor in his bathroom at the assisted living center for an undetermined period of time before staff members came by to check on your parents and found him there, at which point he was already unresponsive. You will know that your mother, in the next room of their small apartment, *had* to have heard him fall, that she *had* to have seen him lying on the floor, that the bathroom door *had* to have been open as it always had been for all sixty-two years of their marriage. You will understand that your mother *didn't* call for help. That she *didn't* push the button. You'll even begin to wonder if it's possible that your mother might have had what she likes to refer to as a "famous screaming match" with your father, a "fight to death," in which she pushed or shoved him while he was unsteadily maneuvering himself in the bathroom with his walker. You will be unsure of which is worse: that you're monstrous enough to have had this thought in the first place, or that no amount of emotional contortions or mental gymnastics will ever allow you to fully *discredit* this thought.

But none of this has happened yet and for now, it is still summer. The Fat Juice is still flowing. And what you *do* know is that by the next morning, your parents will both have seemingly forgotten the ugliness, the rancor, the geriatrically absurd threats of divorce. They will have Eternal Sunshine of the Spotless Mind-ed *all* of it.

And you will be the only one left with this memory.

That slight taste of bile in your mouth.

The sting of something like trapped bees at the back of your throat.

# Space

*Space is the place where I will go when I'm all alone*
*Nobody calls me on the phone and I feel alone*
*Meditating in the zone, all alone*
*Space is the place where I will go*

—"Space is the Place," Sun Ra Arkestra

Christmas Eve, and your neighbor Ruby's dying alone in the apartment across the hall. By your calculations, at the same time Ruby's brain silently hemorrhages—like a supernova swirling into a dark nebula—you're on the phone telling The Beloved you want a time frame for when he's leaving his marriage.

Two months earlier, he'd written a letter to his wife, saying he was moving out, that he wanted a divorce. Since then, he's been carrying the letter around in his pocket, waiting for the right time, he says. But after several weeks, he stops mentioning the letter, and after a month, he becomes prickly and vague every time you ask where things stand. Lately, he's been talking a lot about getting a new tattoo, or trying to "figure out what's going on with the Nigerian poetry scene."

"I'm surprised you haven't asked for a time frame before," he says, which makes you feel dumb, as if poor self-esteem's clinging to your shoe like a soiled clump of toilet paper.

"Well," you say. "I'm asking now."

"It's a reasonable request," he says. You don't care for the way he gets all *business-y* sometimes, as if you're a difficult administrative problem he needs to solve. He's calling you from the parking lot of a Target store somewhere in the large city in the south where he lives. "Let me look at my calendar," he says. "I'll give you a time frame by the end of day tomorrow."

Because it's Christmas and you're apparently more of a sap than you think yourself to be, you mistakenly think The Beloved's time frame is your Christmas present. But when he texts you late at night on Christmas day, you realize he's completely forgotten. *Time frame?!?!* you text. He hesitates, for a very long moment, then texts back *July 1*. Far enough away to preclude immediate action, you think, yet close enough not to totally piss you off. *Date pulled out of your ass?* you text. *No!!!* ☹ ☹ ☹ *!!!* he texts back. But still, you *know* it's a faux date.

Four days later, after you learn Ruby's been discovered dead in her apartment on Christmas day, you ask the landlord for first dibs on her apartment. You don't go so far as to actually say *first dibs*, but it still seems a little crass, particularly by small-town, Midwestern standards. You do it anyway, because you've decided your New Year's resolution is to ask for what you want. Straight up. No rocks.

Several months later, when you move into Ruby's old apartment across the hall, an apartment that—with the exception of the coveted secret attic room—is the mirror image of your former apartment, you feel as if you've turned yourself inside out. Like pulling off a sock.

When the movers you've hired bring over the last of the large furniture, you're unpacking glassware into the kitchen cabinets. "Be careful," one of them says, as you climb down from the step stool to write out a check for him. "In the biz," he says, gesturing at the step stool, "we call those things widow-makers."

Who did Ruby, your former across-the-hall neighbor, make a widow, you wonder? Was it Ruby's decades-long married lover, John, who wasn't there when she died on Christmas Eve? Who wasn't the one who found her on Christmas day? Was he spending the holidays with his family? Did he try to call Ruby from a Target parking lot, wonder why she didn't pick up? Did they have holiday arguments about time frames and transparency? Or, given that Ruby and John were both in their seventies, had these discussions simply become a moot point?

Still, John was devoted to Ruby. You saw his car parked out back most days of the week. When Ruby's health started to go, he brought groceries up to her and drove her to her doctor's appointments. Sometimes you exchanged small talk with him as he cheerfully pruned her lilac bushes.

The irony of moving into Ruby's apartment isn't entirely lost on you. You wonder how The Beloved will find out about your own apparently pending and ignominious death by step stool. Facebook, maybe? If there's no one to widow, you wonder, what do you call the widow-maker? Homefixer? Divine retribution? Reaper? If an adulterer falls in an apartment and there's no one around to hear it, are you still technically alive until someone discovers the body? *Ba dum bum*.

In part, you move because you need something, *anything*, to be different. You move because you need to feel like you're moving on. It's difficult for you to assess, though, in your new inside-out apartment where, weeks later, you keep turning in the wrong direction and bumping into things, if you've ended up *going* anywhere, or if you've merely stepped into the wet concrete of a rapidly hardening future.

You suppose it all depends on how one chooses to interpret the sock. Is a sock turned inside out a sock with fresh possibilities? Or is it just a dirty sock turned inside out?

In the new apartment, you dream The Beloved tells you about his Friday night. He confesses that his wife insists he make dinner for her. But this time, he says, he's refused. He tells his wife he's changed his diet, that he doesn't even like to eat the same things she likes to eat. He won't, he says, make a dinner he's not even going to eat. The Beloved is wearing a white T-shirt and slacks. His feet are bare and propped up as he's telling you this. He shyly says he's proud of himself. He feels like he's making *progress*, he says.

Several days later, you find out that Ruby's married lover, John, was in the hospital with a bad heart over Christmas when Ruby died. You learn he had open heart surgery, and that he didn't make it through.

☾

This is not a ghost story, although there are ghosts. This is not a story about adultery, although there are adulterers. This is a story about meeting your reflection head-on and walking through the looking glass to live on the other side as your Dorian Gray, your Mr. Hyde, your hallucinating Alice.

The first time the radio mounted underneath the kitchen counters comes on, playing Fleetwood Mac's "Second Hand News" in the middle of the night, you're confused, but don't think too much about it. You decide one of the cats must have figured out how to turn on the radio. Maybe the same cat who used to flush the toilet in the old apartment once a night around 2 a.m. The next morning you turn on the radio while you make your morning coffee. It's tuned into a 70s hits station. You imagine that it plays the hits and love songs from when Ruby and John first fell in love. Ruby with her flaming hair, scratchy matchstick laugh. Ruby, the gardener, with her okra patch and honeysuckle bushes that attract the hummingbird-like drone and thrum of sphinx moths on June nights. The clank of Ruby's empty wine bottles clanging into the back-alley dumpsters like the grape-stained tongues of dark bells during the early hours of the morning.

In the new apartment, you dream you're at The Beloved's house, which is next door, where your old apartment used to be. You shouldn't be there. You've accidentally texted him a <3 that you haven't meant to text. It's one of those waking-not-awake dreams. The Beloved's daughters are there. But much older and very busy, with complex needs. The house is a disaster of hoarding. Apparently The Beloved now also has a little boy you didn't know about. The boy wears a striped tank top. He has a mosquito bite on his back. He asks you if you'll scratch it for him. You scratch it gently, between his narrow shoulder blades. His little-boy skin is so tender, though. You don't want to scratch too hard. You ask if there's any chamomile, but given the chaos of the house, this seems like an impossibility. The eldest daughter says there's an old egg in the refrigerator, and that maybe you could hold it against the bite to help cool it down. There are animals everywhere. Cats and dogs and hamsters. Two new cats arrive in boxes from eBay. Someone calls, looking for you. How do they know you're there? You're supposed to be at a studio, being filmed for an interview.

The Beloved leaves with the children, and you fall asleep in a rocking chair propped up by asphalt blocks. You dream that at the interview, the difference between legato and staccato comes up. You demonstrate on a grand piano behind a podium after clearing off inches of dead leaves. After demonstrating staccato, an audience member challenges you on your interpretation of the Bach *Toccata* you've just played. You tell him you studied with a student of Claudio Arrau. But then you wake up from the dream within a dream, and you're in a rocking chair propped up by asphalt blocks in The Beloved's house. The Beloved's wife is standing over you. *Who are you?* she wants to know. *What are you doing in my house?*

Instead of a second-floor balcony, like your old apartment across the hall, the new apartment has a small sunroom off the dining room. You put your desk in this room and work in the treetops, among the birds and squirrels. There are early-morning, late-morning, and afternoon shifts of first grackles, then blue jays, then robins. Even though it's the smallest room in the apartment, you love the openness of the windows, the light, and this is where you spend most of your days. At night, it seems like you're steering the prow of a spaceship into the infinite quiet of dark and unfettered stars.

It's been a dry summer without enough rain. Corn withers on the stalk, and thirsty birds plunder moisture from the fruit of the next-door neighbors' apple trees by piercing their beaks into the apples—like jabbing straws into juice boxes. As June stretches toward July, the apples begin to soften and ferment in the heat, making the birds drunk, so that they sometimes plunk into the sunroom windows like asteroids or other cosmic debris. It makes you feel as if you're in motion, even though you're not. You feel as if you're exploring new frontiers, even though you're not. Still, it's difficult to tell when a body's in rest or a body's in motion in the liminal expanse of space.

☾

In the new apartment, you dream you collide with The Beloved's wife at an academic conference, where she follows you down a hotel corridor and loudly harangues you. The conferees, with their lanyards and briefcases and colorful scarves draped over black turtlenecks, are all staring, and for a moment, you're cringingly mortified. But then you think to yourself, *Fuck it.* You draw yourself up. You're suddenly wearing a lovely stem-green coat with a glamorous fur collar. You stroke the ruff of creamy fur. It's plush and comforting against your fingertips. "I'm a full professor," you inform The Beloved's wife. "I *outrank* you," you say. And then you sashay away to the soundtrack of David Bowie singing "Suffragette City."

You wake up to realize the radio's been turned on in the kitchen again. You wonder if you're trapped inside this inside-out sock of a space. You have the panicky thought that maybe you're somehow stuck, like a skipping record, within the tripped groove of Ruby's life. You take an Ativan and finally fall back to sleep again.

When you wake late the next morning you feel your tangled knot of anxiety slightly ease in the hot buttery stripes of sunlight pastry-brushed through the window blinds. It's the last day of June. You go to the grocery store, where, in the organic foods aisle, you run into a senior colleague who—before Ruby's drinking became an issue—used to be close with Ruby. You tell your friend about the radio. She suggests burning sage in the apartment. When you ask her about John, she tells you he was the love of Ruby's life. That's exactly how your colleague puts it. "He was," she says, "the love of Ruby's life."

Afterwards, when you drive up the alley into the parking space behind your apartment, there's a pair of cardinals on the sidewalk leading to your back door. They are fluttering and hopping excitedly—flash of red and creamy-gray feathers, black masks—around something shiny. You realize the something shiny is a large, iridescent beetle. The male cardinal swoops down and snatches the beetle aloft into his candy-corn orange beak before landing back down on the sidewalk again. He sidles over, scarlet plume quizzically bristling, and offers the beetle to the female cardinal. She steps closer, and for a moment they are beak to beak—the beetle's gleaming green carapace glittering between them in midday sun like shiny foil paper around a wrapped present—and you watch, held breath, as she accepts it.

# Acknowledgments

*Cream City Review*: "But the Psychometric Assumptions of the Tool Were Grossly Violated"

*Green Mountains Review*: "Breakup Blog" and "Date"

*Hairstreak Butterfly Review:* "Belljarred"

*Hotel Amerika:* "Space"

*Midway Journal:* "O, Canada!"

*Midwestern Gothic:* "Semiology"

*Moon City Review:* "Meta/Couch"

*North American Review:* "Amphibious Life" and "Moist Towelette"

*The Offing:* "Reveal Codes"

*Sou'wester:* "Hello Kitty Head"

*Storm Cellar:* "Meditations in an Emergency"

*Story:* "Sundowning, with Fat Juice"

# Moon City Press Short Fiction Award Winners

2014
Cate McGowan
*True Places Never Are*

2015
Laura Hendrix Ezell
*A Record of Our Debts*

2016
Michelle Ross
*There's So Much They Haven't Told You*

2017
Kim Magowan
*Undoing*

2018
Amanda Marbais
*Claiming a Body*

2019
Pablo Piñero Stillmann
*Our Brains and the Brains of Miniature Sharks*

2020
Andrew Bertaina
*One Person Away From You*

2021
Michele Finn Johnson
*Development Times Vary*

2022
Lee Ann Roripaugh
*Reveal Codes*

Printed in the USA
CPSIA information can be obtained
at www.ICGtesting.com
JSHW022301020224
56305JS00006B/26

9 780913 785843